THE

ONLY GIRL

IN TOWN

THE

ONLY GIRL

IN TOWN

ALLY CONDIE

Dutton Books

Dutton Books
An imprint of Penguin Random House LLC, New York

First published in the United States of America by Dutton Books,
an imprint of Penguin Random House LLC, 2023

Dutton is a registered trademark of Penguin Random House LLC.
The Penguin colophon is a registered trademark of Penguin Books Limited.

Visit us online at PenguinRandomHouse.com.

Library of Congress Cataloging-in-Publication Data is available.

ISBN 9780593327173
1st Printing

Printed in the United States of America

LSCH
Edited by Julie Strauss-Gabel
Design by Anna Booth
Text set in Sabon LT Std

For Hope,
for everything.
And for the Game Farm Girls.
It was a gift to run with you.

THE

ONLY GIRL

IN TOWN

1.

now

I am walking back from the water when it happens. I am looking down at my hands in the late-summer sun. It is the time of day when afternoon slides into dusk. I am looking at them, thinking, these are my hands, that is so strange.

My hands are my hands. Like in kindergarten when you have to practice writing your name over and over again until it looks so weird. You start to wonder, *Is this really my name? This can't be my name.* Like a straggle of string unraveled from a sweater, a trail made by a snake in the mud.

I am thinking that and then

I feel the world

empty around me.

Cicadas stop screaming.

Cars stop humming along the road past the edge of the wood.

My phone, which had been buzzing buzzing buzzing in my pocket, goes silent. When I pull it out, it's cold and dead. When I turn it on, there is no signal.

In the distance, the water splashes over the spillway, but no one calls or cries out.

I know before I know

that everyone is gone.

2.

now

Just your mind, my brain says. *Just your mind playing tricks on you. Everyone's not gone. The world's not empty. That's impossible. Get in the car. Go home. Everything will be fine.*

I've made it through the woods and I'm standing where we leave our cars when we go to the jump. Parked under a heavy-branched tree is my beat-up old Subaru. Silver. Long scratch on the driver's side door and an old, peeling KEEP LITHIA GREEN bumper sticker on the back.

But there is no sense of coming and leaving. No engines turning off or on, no crunch of footsteps in the gravel of the parking area, no people calling out to one another in greeting or farewell.

I unlock the car and get in and lock it.

The car is hot and muggy inside, an empty Gatorade bottle rattling around in the front seat where Sam or Sydney or Alex or Ella or Jack used to sit.

I hear my friends laughing. I see Sam turn his head to look at me, the lights from the dashboard illuminating his face. The air rushes in through the windows and it smells of summer rain.

I turn away from the memories and put my hands on the steering wheel. Then my forehead against it.

Breathe, I say.

Just your mind.

3.

now

I send a message to everyone in my contacts. The message says:

Hello?

I wait.

Nothing, no one writes back.

4.

now

Not a single other car on the road.
    No one out with their dog
    walking across the yard with a plate of cookies for their
neighbor
    pushing a lawnmower into the garage
    talking at the mailbox
    the curb
    the little park at the end of the road.
    No kids playing in the yard
    or runners on the street
    or teenagers walking together in knots on the sidewalks.
    Not a soul along the wide grassy areas by the college dorms.

5.

now

I drive, slowly, down the street.

There is no screen-blue light seeping through windows. Nobody playing in their yards. No snick-hiss of backyard sprinklers, no smell of burgers grilled for dinner in the air.

I get out of the car and go up the sidewalk to my house.

My heart tick-tocks with hope.

Someone has to be there.

They can't all

be gone.

6.

now

The dishes sit on the table, clean. The chairs are tucked in nice and neat.

My brother, Jack, would never leave his that way. He's always on his way to a baseball game or a night out with friends or a morning practice and so his chairs are left askew, his sentences are half-finished, his life is *in medias res* all the time.

"Hey?" I call out. "Mom? Dad? Jack?"

I check all the rooms, the closets, under all the beds, in the backyard, the side yard, the front yard.

It's like they haven't been here for a long time.

But they were just here.

Weren't they?

I look down at my phone.

Still nothing.

From anyone.

7.

Therapist: *You should make a list.*

July: *Of what?*

Therapist: *Of ways to calm yourself. To settle the weather pattern in your head.*

July: *I don't—*

July:

Therapist: *You don't what?*

July: *See how that's going to help.*

Therapist: *You don't have to do it now. That can be your homework, okay? Bring it with you next time.*

8.

now

Think.

In the event of a disaster, our neighborhood's designated meeting place is supposed to be the high school. Maybe that's where everyone went, and they just forgot me.

Back when we were little, my parents did that to Jack once; they forgot him at a picnic table in Hopkins Glen State Park. We turned the car around, my dad on the phone to 911 and my mom crying. When we got back to the park, Jack was exactly where we'd left him, except surrounded by people and eating a piece of chocolate cake with buttercream frosting from someone's birthday party that they'd been celebrating at a nearby table.

Both my parents' cars are in the garage.

Maybe they walked, I tell myself.

My car waits out front. When I turn it on, the radio is nothing but static.

9.

now

The parking lot at Lithia High School is empty. Every door is locked. I tried them all. Front doors, back doors, gym doors, doors I've never noticed before. I peer in through the windows: vacant rooms. I circle back to the front of the building again, to the marquee out on the main lawn.

This is where we always met for our cross-country training runs. In the summer mornings, after school when classes started up again.

Technically, the cross-country teams have Fridays off in the summers. But the runners who really want to be good, they come anyway.

We do this long run called the Fall Creek Run on Fridays. Eight miles. It's a monster. You start here at the high school, and then you run up a huge hill, through the gorge. Then out past the farms, up another hill, circle back and come down past the Howell University horse pastures, and then down Fall Creek Road. About a mile before we get back to the high school, we cut through the wildflower preserve to the pond above the spillway on Fall Creek.

And that's where we jump.

Someone on the girls' team started the tradition years ago. Then the guys joined in. College kids do it, too, but not early in the morning like us. One of them died at the jump a few years ago. You can see the white cross his friends made for him when you're coming along the path. He was drunk.

Other people have died there, but not everyone gets a cross.

We're like the opposite of drunk when we jump. We've been running for miles by the time we're leaping from the cliffs into the water just above the spillway. Once you make the jump on one of the Fall Creek Fridays, you're part of the team. It's our rite of passage.

It feels so good. The water is so cold. Then we get back out and run the last mile back to school. Right back here.

Lithia High doesn't have enough money for one of those electric marquees like other schools have. We've got an ancient sign with plastic letters that the student government officers have to change by hand whenever it's time for a new announcement or event. On the coldest, worst days, when we were out there freezing, trying to get those damn letters up on the board without dropping them, we cursed the cheapness of the school district, the fact that we'd ever signed up for this in the first place, the whole thing.

The last time I noticed, the marquee said HAVE A GOOD SUMM3R, the way it had for weeks. There was only one *E*, so the student body officers always ended up having to use *3*s instead.

But now, those words are gone.

Instead, a date.

8/31.

My heart is tick-tocking harder than ever.

Who did this?

My hands begin to shake.
Who put this up?
How long has it been here?
Did it happen before
or after
everyone disappeared?

10.

WAYS TO BE OKAY

- *Run.*
- *Read.*
- *Watch a show that makes you laugh.*
- *Make something.*
- *Help someone.*
- *Create a playlist.*
- *Hot chocolate.*
- *Warm baths.*
- *Pet your cat. Or your dog.*
- *Walk barefoot in the grass.*
- *Go for a long drive on a long road and listen to music. A really good song, an angry one or a sad one or a good beat one, one that matches the rhythm of what you're feeling inside and brings it outside, so you can hear and scream and sing. Songs like that are like a handhold on a slick wall, something you can hold on to with all your might for as long as it lasts.*
- *Wrap up in a blanket and lie on the floor and tell yourself, "I don't have to do anything. I don't have to go anywhere. I don't have to be anyone. I am just a person in a blanket on the floor."*

11.

now

Maybe it's only people in Lithia who've vanished. There's plenty of gas in the Subaru, so I head through downtown and toward Route 13, which snakes around the lake.

I'll try Nicholsburg, the next town over.

I drive over a bridge.

A thing you should know about our town is that it is cut through, divided.

With rivers, gorges.

Rich people, poor people.

College kids, townies.

I come down the dip on the highway that leads to Tanner Falls, right outside the Lithia town limits. There is *always* someone at the falls, even in the winter. People snowshoe and cross-country ski the trail; they take photographs of the water all year long. Frozen. Thawed. Spring flow, summer swimming. And it's a perfect evening right now, prime time for people to gather. I can practically *see* a dad with a baby in a carrier, a woman with a dog, a group of teenagers in cutoff shorts and swimsuits, a family with a picnic, everyone packing up or staying to feel the last of the light. They'll be there. For sure.

So what if there are no other cars on the road, either coming or going? It means I can floor it and get there faster.

I come down to the lowest part of the hill, to where it's

about to swell back up. I don't even care who I see first, whether I know them or not, I am going to throw my arms around them and hold the hell on.

But.

The car is no longer moving, even though I'm pressing—*hard*—on the gas.

There's no wall, invisible or visible, nothing I've hit, but I can't go forward, or see past the rise in the road.

I can *hear* the waterfall, the low sing of it audible now that almost every other sound is gone.

I pull the car over. I put it in park and get out.

I try to walk up the road instead of drive.

Same thing.

I can't move forward.

It is very, *very* weird to walk and walk and not gain any ground at all. I feel like I'm walking in place, the same terrain cycling beneath me like I'm on a treadmill.

Maybe it's just the road. The road has a problem. I can still get through. I can still find my way to the falls and to people, to a spot outside of my town.

I make my way into the forest, past the tangle of bushes that lines the road and into the deep green shade of the trees. Somewhere in this forest is the border between Lithia and the rest of the world. On the road, it's clear where that boundary is, but in the woods, not so much. Leaves cover the ground, thick, and I have to push through the bushes and branches.

Maybe there's a secret path. Maybe I can trick whatever it is that's done this, and it won't see me if I'm not on the road.

All I have to do is try hard enough, and I'll find my way out.

12.

Therapist: *Did you make your list? The one of ways to be okay?*

July: *Yes, I did.*

Therapist: *Would you like to share it with me? You don't have to.*

July: *Okay. [reads list out loud, except the last item]*

Therapist: *That's a great list. Did it feel helpful?*

July: *Sure.*

July:

Therapist:

Therapist: *Okay. Let's keep going. Did you happen to try the mock interview exercise I recommended?*

July: *I'm sorry. The what?*

Therapist: *The exercise where you imagine you're sitting with everyone you'd like to talk to, and you're asking them all the questions you want to ask? And letting them answer?*

July: *Oh. Right. Yes, I tried it.*

Therapist: *What did you think?*

July: *It was nice.*

Therapist: *Can you help me understand what you mean by "nice"?*

July: *I don't know.*

Therapist:

July:

Therapist: *Okay. Let me try another question. Were you able to picture those conversations in a way that was helpful for you?*

July: *I mean, that's the problem, right? That's what makes it impossible to trust the conversations. The interviews. Because it's all there.*

Therapist: *Where?*

July: *In my head.*

13.

now

I'm pushing through the forest, and at last I break into a clearing. Not even a clearing, really, but a small space without any undergrowth. Just a spot of long grass starred with a few flowers and something . . . else. I point my phone's light down so I can see better in the dusk.

A . . . notebook?

It's open. I reach down to touch it and pull my hand back as if it's been bitten by a snake.

It's my *journal.*

How did it get here?

I threw it into the water.

No one saw me do it.

And I'm not anywhere near where I threw it. I'm clear on the other side of town.

I reach out again and pick up the journal.

It's swollen, ruined, all of the pages illegible. Waterlogged, then dried out, now damp again from the grass.

It's fallen open to a certain spot. A sprig of leaves has been stuck inside like a bookmark.

And over what I had once written, what I can no longer read, someone

has scrawled
their handwriting almost illegible:
GET
THEM
BACK.

14.

once

When we came running into the parking lot at the entrance to the trail, Sam was standing by his car, a beat-up old black Jeep. He was even better-looking than I'd remembered him from Verity, and he had that good-guy look that I like—kind eyes, great smile. Plus: dark hair, broad shoulders, dimple.

I couldn't believe he was here.

Two days before, he'd taken my order at Verity Ice Cream. He'd asked for my number when I'd finished up and we'd been texting ever since. On a whim, I'd told him about the run.

"Wow," Syd said under her breath. Sam noticed her, because guys always did, but his eyes slid right over to meet mine. Ella stopped a few feet behind us, shy.

Good things usually happened to Syd. But this time it wasn't for her. Sam was for *me*.

"So what exactly are we doing?" Sam asked, taking a step in my direction. "Jumping off a cliff?"

"Yup," I said. He wore shorts and a T-shirt and flip-flops. His eyes were bright blue and his hair was a just-woke-up tangle of dark brown.

I saw him look, take me in. My T-shirt, stuck to my chest, my legs, my ponytail, the way the sun hit my hair, the sweat on my skin.

"Is this legal?" he asked.

"It's public property," I said as we threaded our way down the trail, Syd leading out, Ella looking over her shoulder with a thrilled expression, Sam and me behind.

"That's not an answer," he said.

"No, it's not," I agreed. "Follow me."

Lacy tangles of white flowers brushed our legs, and I ran my hand along the tops of the yellow and purple ones that bordered the path. The grass on the trail smelled sweet and full. We had to go single file, so I went ahead of Sam.

I felt strong and alive and knew I would always be both.

We came to the cliff and stood there, looking down at the pool above the spillway. Alex and Colton and some of the other guys had beaten us there and were already jumping, one after another after another. People had taken off their T-shirts and abandoned them in clusters at the top, draped over branches. The people who'd already jumped were swimming to the edge of the spillway and leaning over it, talking, the water going past them, down Fall Creek, and all the way to Cayuga Lake.

"It's higher up than I thought," Ella said, sounding nervous. She was young, just a freshman. I'd been giving her a ride to practice since the first week, when I'd noticed her walking all the way down to the high school from her house.

Sam stayed next to me on the slate-colored rock, the two of us looking down.

The water was deep emerald green, the color of a wine bottle, a tangle of jungle leaves, a piece of velvet slumped in a display window with old books scattered across it. Later today, when the heat came up, there would be bodies all over the rocks and the small sandy beach below—suntanned college and graduate students who had stuck around for the summer, and townies like us.

It wasn't crowded now, but at first I wanted them all gone, even the girls from the team, even my friends, even Syd and Alex.

I wanted them all gone.

But then I realized that people were seeing Sam, and me, and in a way it was even better than if we'd been alone.

Sam pulled off his flip-flops. I knew he was getting ready to jump, so I did it first. I heard Alex cheering when I went over.

The water tasted cold, like old stone and moss. Even in the summer, it was still so chilly it took my breath away. My body slipped through, went under, and I opened my eyes against the deep green. I stayed down as long as I dared.

When I came back up, Sam had already jumped in and come to the surface. He was looking for me. I swam away from the group, around the corner of the rock cliff, where the others couldn't see us, and when I looked back, I saw that he had caught sight of me and was following, long smooth strokes against the water.

My feet hit the bottom near the shore, and I stood up. So did Sam. My hair was in my eyes and I pushed it away. His body was slick and wet and I thought about my T-shirt, sitting in the sun at the top of the cliff, and how it would feel to put it back on after being so cold. My sports bra would soak right through it, but the cotton would be warm on my skin. I thought these things so I wouldn't think about Sam, but when he took a step closer, that became impossible.

Neither of us was smiling.

It felt like we were balancing on the knife's edge of something bigger than we were, something we couldn't control.

"Let me give you some advice about Lithia," I said. "This town is beautiful. But be careful where you jump."

15.

now

I'm back at my house. I open the door, praying.

Please. This time let it be different.

Please.

"Hello?"

Nothing, no one says back.

Okay. Okay.

Maybe this is a dream.

It's not, I know it's not.

Maybe I'm dead.

I'm not, I know I'm not.

The framed family photo on the wall is from last fall. The new bed we bought for our cat, Yolo, because he'd torn up his old one, is sitting in front of the fireplace.

We all thought it was super funny when we named our cat Yolo.

Because it stands for "you only live once" and cats have nine lives. Get it?

They don't actually have to worry about YOLO.

I keep walking around the house. The bedspread in my parents' room is the one they got this spring. Jack's summer league team picture is up on his bulletin board.

I have the long thin scar on my forearm where a stick dragged across me sharp and neat when I was hiking earlier this summer, in June.

I still have all the marks from the last year. On the outside of me, and inside. I feel them. It's still today.

I don't think I'm dreaming

or dead

or trapped in the past.

Just

alone.

16.

once

We stood with our hands behind our heads, fingers threaded together, trying to catch our breath. The sun slanted green-gold through the trees around the high school, and the air was muggy and cooler than usual from the rain the night before. The green bushes that lined the parking lot dripped with water, and I could smell the earth, lush and ripe.

"Nice run," Coach Warren said.

"Thanks," Syd said. I was still catching my breath.

"I've got some good news for you two," Coach said. "The other girls voted you as team captains for the year."

"Aw," Syd said. "That's so sweet." She seemed pleased, and not surprised.

I was, though. "Wow," I said. "That's awesome."

But who else did I think it would be?

17.

now

I lock all the doors.

What is going on?

The date on the marquee.

The words in my journal.

How did it get there?

And when?

And who wrote in it?

I race up the stairs to my parents' bedroom, lock that door, too. I drag the comforter and a pillow off their bed and go into their bathroom. I lock *that* door and then crawl into the space underneath the built-in vanity. The tile is hard and cold and gray. I close my eyes.

18.

once

This is my earliest concrete memory.

We are driving late at night. It is me and my mom and dad and Jack who is three years old. I am five.

It is late and I am so tired. I am crying.

The night's dark.

Something is scaring me.

I don't know what it is.

It's bigger than a monster, wider than an ocean.

It's everywhere.

Outside me.

Inside me.

I'm crying and Jack's asleep but he won't be for long if I keep this up. "July, honey, it's okay," my mom says. "Please stop crying. Sweetie. You're going to wake up your brother."

She tries to tell me the story of my birth, which I've always liked. How I was due on the Fourth of July but I came so early, in May instead. How they were worried about me but I was a fighter. How they decided to keep the name they'd picked for me—July—even though I came in May. Because I was a firecracker from the start. I lit up the sky.

But I can't stop crying.

I'm too scared.

Mom has Dad pull the car over. She climbs in the back, in between our two booster seats.

"It's okay," she says. "It's okay."

She picks up my sippy cup and says my name into it. "JULY." She's trying to get through to me, to have me hear her in a different way, and it almost works. I stop for a second. But the fear is still there, and I start to cry again.

My mom keeps saying my name, very gently. She doesn't lose her temper, she doesn't put the cup down. She starts singing my name into it. Then she turns my name into a song.

I listen.

Ju-ly, Ju-ly Fielding.
Ju-ly, Ju-ly Fielding.
Ju-ly, Ju-ly Fielding, Ju-ly, Fielding,
is a pretty name.
Ju-ly, Ju-ly Fielding.
Ju-ly, Ju-ly Fielding.
Ju-ly, Ju-ly Fielding, Ju-ly, Fielding,
you will be okay.

19.

now

I wake, sitting bolt upright, and slam my head against the bottom of the vanity.

What am I doing under my parents' vanity?

Crap. Right.

I'm the last person left in town, and I'm sleeping under a vanity because I got scared by a date on a marquee and a message in my old journal. I've gone to ground like an animal.

A thought nudges at my mind. *Where* are *all the animals?* I didn't hear the buzz of insects last night. There are no birds chirping the way they always do in the morning.

Have they gone, too?

Is anyone back yet?

I grab my phone and lie down again.

Nothing. No texts. But the date on the display has changed. One day forward.

So, time is moving. We're going to get closer to the 8/31 date. It's going to be 8/31 again.

The numbers on the marquee don't mean that, I tell myself. *Not necessarily. Remember, it could just be the time everything stopped.*

One of my mom's eyeliner pencils is on the floor under the sink with me. She must have dropped it. The shade is one she used to wear a couple of years ago—brown, not black. Without getting up, without lifting my head, I pick up the pencil and make a mark on the underside of the vanity like a prisoner would. A notch.

I have that sick feeling you get when you wake up and you know something bad has happened. And you have to remember what it is.

But I've already remembered that I'm alone. That everyone else is gone. What more could there be?

I crawl out and stand, yanking up the blind and looking through the bathroom window at the tangle of mint and thyme in the herb garden along the fence, at the trees in the yard. Empty. I push open the window. Nothing. Still no sound.

I have to find someone.

20.

My therapist handed me a Post-it. Fluorescent pink. I've always hated neon colors. My mom bought me a hot-pink T-shirt when I was little, and I would never wear it, not even once. I told her, "I don't like that color! It's screaming at my eyes!"

"Write down the names of the most important people to you," my therapist said. She handed me a black Sharpie pen, fine point. That, I liked. It was so smooth across the paper.

"Do you need to see the names?" I asked her when I finished. I wondered if she'd say, "Who on earth do you know that is named Yolo?" and then I would say, "It's my cat," and if she would try to tell me that a cat was not a person.

But she said no. Instead, she asked, "What does this list tell you?"

I knew she wanted me to say something like, these are the people I love who love me back and they're the only people whose opinions matter. So that's what I said, and she liked it.

"Does it help?" she asked me.

I knew she wanted me to say yes it does so I said that.

"Good," she said. "You can put it with your list of ways to be okay."

Yes, yes, I nodded, showing her I understood and would for

sure and definitely do that. I would put both the ways to be okay list and the people who love me list on my mirror so I could see them every day. Absolutely. Of course.

I did not tell her that the lists never really worked.

Or that maybe I had never been okay.

21.

now

I know where Alex's family keeps their spare key. It's in a fake rock in the backyard flower bed. I push away the heavy-leaved peony plants, their blossoms gone since June. My fingers are dappled with still-clinging dew, though the sun on my back is already hot. Their dog, Bo, would absolutely be barking his way toward me right now if things were normal, but all I hear is the snick-snack of me sliding open the secret compartment in the rock to get the key.

It's not breaking into someone's house if everyone in town has disappeared and you have to find out what happened. Like, if ever there were extenuating circumstances, that's what's happening here.

Near the back steps, there is a tangle of Queen Anne's lace that Alex's mom likes to keep wild because she uses it in floral arrangements. She's a nurse and very clean, so everything else, inside and outside of the house, is shipshape and tidy. I put the key in the lock and push it open and head straight for their kitchen.

It's the same as my house. No plates on the table. Chairs tucked in. A framed photo of Alex, his parents, and his sister visiting family in India sits neatly on the sideboard where it's always been. Cookbooks line the kitchen shelves, not a one out of place.

"Hey?" I call out. "Alex?"

I hear a creak upstairs and my heart thumps with fear and excitement. I should have come straight here last night, when everything first happened. I shouldn't have let the marquee freak me out. I pound up the stairs two at a time, rounding the corner to Alex's room.

Alex Dhawan and I became best friends in seventh grade. We both played saxophone in middle school band. We bonded over how bad we were. We were so bad the band teacher asked us not to return the next year. We weren't even mad. We understood.

It feels like snooping to actually look inside the drawers of Alex's desk or his dresser. There's a stack of notebooks on the corner of his desk, the black-and-white composition kind. I don't open one, but I know what I'd see if I did—lines and lines of his oddly beautiful handwriting in fine-point black Sharpie, his favorite kind of pen. I don't see his phone anywhere. I do see the set of mini-golf clubs I gave him as kind of a joke one year. We always went mini-golfing on the Fourth of July at National Wonders, this awesomely crappy place at the edge of town. The people who built it were obsessed with national parks. So each hole represents a different park. And if you get a hole in one at Yellowstone, you get a free pass for the next time.

Creak.

The sound, again.

I look around Alex's room for something I could use to defend myself. I pick up one of the clubs, though it wouldn't be much defense against an intruder. And at this point I might actually welcome an intruder. Another living, breathing human being.

I hear the sound a third time.

A creak, a pop.

I recognize it now.

It's only the floorboards, expanding in the heat.

22.

once

When I was eight, the toilet in the bathroom next to my bedroom started making a weird whiny sound at night.

It was the most lonesome sound in the world.

Like a sad, aching, cosmic wail. Not made by anything alive. It sounded like it was made by something older than alive.

It made me think of stars and how big the universe was.

It made me think of how small I was.

In my mind, I called it the cold lonely sound.

"What happens when we die?" I asked my mom one night when she came to tuck me in.

She sat down on the bed. "Oh, honey," she said. "Do you want me to tell you what some people believe? Or do you want me to tell you what I think is the truth?"

"The truth," I said.

"Well," she said. "We're very, very lucky to be born at all. Do you know how strange and beautiful it is to be living?"

I did. I felt that. I had always felt that.

"The odds against all the ancestors over all the years meeting up and having the children they did, and the odds against the exact cells coming together to make you . . ."

"I know," I said. That part was awesome and scared me, too.

"Right," she said. "You're asking about dying. Not being born."

I waited. I had a stuffed fox that had once been hers, from a movie when she was small. I was holding on to it tight.

"I think we're part of nature," my mom said gently. "We're born, and we live, and then we die. And our bodies return to the earth. Things grow from it again. So we're always a part of the universe."

She kissed my forehead.

I held on tight to that fox, even though it was not alive, even though it had never been alive, and I did not sleep.

23.

now

"You didn't stay drowned," I tell my journal. I threw it in the lake at the end of last summer. "But *this* should do the trick."

I light it on fire in my driveway with the matches my mom keeps next to the stove.

I let it lick, lick, lick.

Eat, eat, eat.

Burn, burn, burn.

Until all the pages are shriveled up black and gone.

This time, for good.

It's almost night again. I have been alone for twenty-four hours. I have knocked on the doors of almost everyone I know, like some kind of crazed salesman or missionary who has pest control or religion to share. But no one answered. When I peered into windows, no one looked back.

And now I'm home again. Burning.

Something comes over me. A feeling. Like I'm floating flat on my back in a dark cold lake, staring at the sky, and I know there's a swim of things going on underneath that could take me down.

Despair.

I burned the journal.

So what?

Now what?

I leave the ashes on the driveway and walk over to the front steps to sit down. It's humid, the air weighing on me like a hand, pressing against every inch of my skin. Along the road, one of the streetlights flickers on, then out. I watch for a minute, but it stays dark. Maybe I imagined it.

I used to sit here with Yolo in my lap, his sleek black fur and purr a warm silk.

I wish I had my cat back.

My words hang in the lonely, unbreathing night.

24.

now

And

Something leaps and lands, soft but solid, on the porch next to me.

Yolo.

He's back.

25.

now

My cat is back.

Yolo climbs onto my lap and purrs and kneads, as if he's been waiting for this for ages, too.

He's always acted like that. Like he'd been *soooo* neglected, even if I'd hung out with him moments before.

I'm laughing and crying. I'm hugging him so hard he gives me a *meh* of annoyance.

He was always too lazy to do the full meow, just the *meh*, and that's how I am one hundred percent sure that it is him. He sticks his claws into my knee and lifts his chin so I can get the soft spot under it, the spot where he has a secret gray patch that's usually hidden.

Yolo is back.

"Such a good boy," I say, "such a good boy you are," and he *meh*s at me again and I'm so delighted. And then I realize:

oh my gosh.

oh my gosh I think I wished Yolo back.

26.

now

Wait.

What.

Is that what this is?

Is *this* how I get them back?

Yolo is *meh*ing at me, walking away, and I jump up to follow—I am not letting him out of my sight, I will stalk him as tenaciously as he used to stalk the neighbor's Chihuahua. Yolo pauses at the back door, waiting for me to let him in, and when I do, he goes straight to the pantry where we keep the cat food and waits for me to pour him out a bowl. *"Meh,"* he says again when I've finished, and it makes me laugh again.

Could it be this easy?

Do I just have to wish?

Wishes aren't science. They make zero sense. But neither does a whole town vanishing around you.

I open my mouth to say every name I can as fast as I can, but a *meh* from Yolo stops me. He's watching me.

"You're right," I tell him. "I should think this through."

What if I've only got three? Like a fairy tale?

But even though I'm a girl talking to her cat like a princess in a castle, this is no fairy tale. I'm trapped and I can't get out, but I'm not asleep, and no prince is at the gates thinking he can save me.

I have to be careful.

27.

once

Sam texted *I'm stuck at work all night come see me*
and I texted back
I can't
I'm babysitting the Miller kids overnight for the first time
and Sam wrote back
Bring them
Kids like ice cream

I looked at the kids, who were sitting in a circle in the family room, three towheads waiting for me to keep playing duck, duck, goose with them.

"Let's take a break," I said. "How about we go get ice cream?"

"But it's almost bedtime," Annie said, looking thrilled. She was the youngest, five years old.

"We'll be fast," I promised.

They rocketed to their feet and ran off in search of flip-flops or sandals. I gathered up the pillows and blankets they'd scattered from a fort we'd made earlier.

The Millers' house was one of those perfect family houses. The kind with hardwood floors and rain jackets hanging on pegs; snickerdoodle or chocolate chip cookies in a Tupperware on the counter; white lights hanging over a weathered back patio full of plants in pots; soccer balls dotting the backyard. The family room had a fireplace and shelves filled with books; kids' paintings hung on the fridge and were tacked to bulletin boards. There was a fresh laundry smell, rosebushes and flagstones in the yard. It was a beautiful home but one that was worn at the edges. You wanted to live there, not tiptoe through it and tell your friends about it later. The Millers had moved in that winter, and the house already felt like they had been there forever.

"Where are we going to get the ice cream?" Annie asked, as they piled into the car.

"Verity," I said, sliding into the driver's seat. The Millers had one of those SUVs with two rows of seats in the back. It was very new and very shiny, and it always made me nervous to drive it.

"We're never been to Verity!" Kate said from what they called the back-back-seat. She was the oldest, nine.

"Seriously?" I asked. Verity Ice Cream is a Lithia institution. It's been around since the 1930s.

"We haven't lived here very long," Drew, the middle kid, reminded me. His dad, Jake, had gotten a job as a professor at Howell University. Hannah, the mom, worked at a nonprofit.

"I'll have to show you all the good Lithia summer stuff," I said. "Ice cream. Peach pancakes at Zippy's Diner. Sandwiches at Home Run Deli. Hiking in Hopkins Glen. S'mores. Lakeside Park. Catching fireflies. Berry picking. Swimming."

"We go to the swimming pool all the time," Kate said. "At the country club."

"Well, I've never been to the country club," I said.

"Really?"

"Really." My parents did okay—my mom was a dental hygienist and my dad was a graphic designer—but joining the country club was not a thought that would have ever crossed either of their minds. "And there are lots of secret swimming places besides the regular pools. Ponds, and spots in the state parks."

"Really?" Annie had gone breathless. "*Secret* swimming pools?"

"Can you take us there?" Drew asked.

"I'll have to check with your parents first."

Finding some of the secret swimming spots had been something I'd done with Alex the summer after ninth grade. He and I always invented a project for the summer. One year, we'd learned the butterfly stroke in swimming.

This year, we were trying every flavor on the menu at Verity Ice Cream together.

I started driving down the road that snaked from the Heights—the Millers' old, beautiful neighborhood—to downtown. "But you're going to love this ice cream. I promise. They have a ton of flavors."

The summer evening crowd was out in full force. We had to wait in line, and I read the flavors of ice cream listed on the giant blackboard over and over to each of the kids while they decided. Sam was there, wearing his work uniform, a white button-up short-sleeved shirt and a red baseball cap with the Verity logo on it. I kept having to look away because I wanted him to come out from behind the counter and put his mouth on mine and I was worried that that was showing on my face.

When it was finally our turn, we ended up with another employee helping us because Sam was already busy. I was either going to crack up laughing from the faked formality of the whole thing or implode with lust the next time I caught his eye. I got Cinnamon Crunch because it was a flavor I'd already had with Alex so I wouldn't be breaking our pact. Kate got Mint Chocolate Chip, and the younger two both got Bubble Gum Blast. I knew I'd have to keep an eye on where all that gum ended up.

We sat at one of the picnic tables outside, sharing it with a young mom and her baby in a stroller. She was feeding him vanilla ice cream from a tiny sample spoon, and every time she gave him a bite, he kicked his legs in delight.

I went over to get extra water cups for the kids to save their bubble gum chunks in for later. It was disgusting, but it was also what Jack and I had done as kids. No way would we ever have let all that gum go to waste. As I was walking toward the door, a car drove by and someone wolf-whistled me, and I flipped them off before I remembered that the kids might be watching.

When I came back, the younger two had chipmunk cheeks full of gum that they'd been saving up while they waited for me. They spat them into their cups and wiped their mouths with red-and-white napkins printed with the Verity slogan: *Truly Delicious.*

A loose knot of teenagers sat at a table next to us, flirting and laughing and telling jokes. The kids watched them in fascination.

"We are up *so late*," Annie whispered, almost to herself, in total delight.

Sam came outside to bring someone at another table a banana split. The whipped cream was already starting to slide off the top because he'd put on too much. I stood up to get another cup of water for Annie. After Sam delivered the ice cream, he walked over to where I was standing at the spigot. Without either of us saying anything, we ducked around the corner. He pulled me in and kissed me fast, so quick it left me breathless. He tasted like ice cream, blackberry.

"Hey," he said.

"Hey," I said back.

I closed my eyes. His lips were so good. Both of our hands were on each other's backs, just under the hems of each other's shirts, our fingers grazing each other's skin. Every part of me was singing and I knew this was the best anyone could ever feel.

"I'd better get back," I whispered. We both held on for a second longer before I pulled away and walked toward the kids.

I knew he was watching me go.

28.

now

Okay. Think.

"I'm going to be smart about this," I tell Yolo.

Everyone knows what happens when people in stories get wishes. They end up wasting them. It happens literally every time.

And I'm no different. If I do only have three, I've already kind of wasted one, wishing on Yolo.

Yolo full-out *meows* at me, and he sounds pissed, like he read my mind.

"No offense," I say. "You're the first animal I'd wish back. For sure. And you'd be ahead of most people."

That thought thuds my heart. *But not* all *people.* There are some I want back so badly I feel like I'm clawing my way through every hour every minute every second without them.

Be careful. Think. Don't get emotional. Yet.

Plus, what if I get greedy? What if I wish for the whole town back, and it's too much for, like, the wishing system? What if there are limits? What if there aren't?

Okay. To start, I should wish for something bigger than Yolo. A single person. See if that works.

If it does, then I'll wish for the town. And if *that* works, then

I'll see if I have another wish. Maybe it's not limited to three. Maybe the possibilities are endless.

I mean, if an entire town can disappear, anything can happen. Right?

29.

once

"Listen up," Syd said. "Here are the rules."

Someone in the group huddled under the marquee was still talking. "I'm sorry," Syd said, shining her phone's flashlight on a startled-looking freshman boy. "Did *you* need to say something to the rest of us?"

Even in the weak beam, I could see him blushing. He looked both terrified and thrilled by her attention. "No, no," he said, and another boy started laughing and muttered something. Syd moved her light to him, and he froze, too.

She waited. Until everything was perfectly quiet. Until you could hear a pin drop.

"We're playing hide and seek," Syd said. "Our way."

Fall Creek Fridays weren't the only informal tradition that team captains were responsible for carrying on. Sometimes we'd send out texts telling the team members to meet for random activities. All-you-can-eat night at the Pasta House. A movie at the ancient drive-in. And, at least once every summer: night games.

Syd and Alex had sent the text to both teams: *MEET AT MARQUEE. 9 P.M.*

"As I was saying," she said. "Hide and seek. The rules. You can hide anywhere on the school grounds. *Outside.* With anyone you want to, from either team. Bonus points for making out."

Syd always made everything a bit extra. That had never been part of the rules before.

"Syd," I said, but she pretended not to hear me.

"How is whoever's It going to find everyone else?" someone asked. "The grounds are huge."

"Once you get found, you'll start looking, too," Alex said. "So pretty soon there's a lot more than one person looking."

"There's a point where it's actually scarier *not* to be found," Syd said. "When you're out there in the dark, and you know more and more people are hunting for you."

Two of the freshman girls shivered in fear.

"You," Syd said, pointing to the boy who'd been talking earlier. "You're It."

He turned around obediently and began to count.

"Louder!" Syd said. "We've got to be able to hear you."

He raised his voice, and we all took off.

The high school fields were wide and green and ran into each other, lacrosse and soccer and baseball, different white lines sprayed onto the grass. Where to go? I was giddy, the stars were bright pinpricks of light. The smell of grass surrounded me and my breath came fast. I saw a shadow as Syd and I sprinted along the edge of the chain-link fence.

"Baseball dugout," she said, reading my mind. We raced toward it, shooting across the field and into the concrete structure. Inside, it was pitch-black.

"Uh-oh," Syd said. "We've got a follower."

"What?" I asked, confused.

She jerked her head at a figure racing across the baseball diamond toward us. It took me a moment to recognize the shape.

Ella.

"Sorry!" Ella stopped a couple of steps away, didn't sit down on the bench next to us. Her whisper carried into the cool concrete enclosure. "I didn't plan to follow you guys! But I couldn't think of anywhere to go and I panicked!"

"It's totally fine," I said, grabbing her hand and pulling her closer to us.

"If anyone saw you coming, we're dead." Syd tucked herself farther back into the corner.

"I don't think anyone did." Ella sounded chagrined.

At that very moment, Syd let out a long, froggy, absolutely-on-purpose belch.

"Syd," I hissed, but a guffaw was bubbling up in my throat. Next to me, I could feel Syd shaking with suppressed laughter, her arm right up against mine.

And there is nothing funnier than laughing when you're not supposed to laugh. On my other side, Ella began to giggle.

"Shut up shut up shut up," Syd said, but she was still laughing, too.

"I saw someone come over here." A voice. Male. The boy who was It.

We all went silent in an instant.

He was close. Closer. I could hear the scuff of his shoes. And the thrill of almost being found, the sheer terror of being discovered in the night, of waiting, brushed a chill along my back. I held my breath.

Three girls in the dark, hearts pounding.

"Do. Not. Move." Syd whispered, so quiet that I didn't even know if I heard it, or if I just knew what she would say. The three of us sat rigid on the bench, playing rigor-mortis dead. Would the boys' eyes adjust to the dark? I felt like our sneakers, our teeth, our bones inside us, were all gleaming white, asking to be found in spite of ourselves.

"Okay," Ella whispered, out of nowhere. Her voice was so soft I could barely hear it. "I've got this."

Fast as a shot, as if a starting gun had fired, she darted out of the dugout.

"Hey!" The kid took off after Ella, who was making good time across the grass.

"Oh my gosh," Syd said. "What is she thinking? This isn't tag."

"Maybe she's going to hide again."

"She can't outrun him." Syd was probably right. Even the average guys were almost always faster than the fastest girls. It was patently unfair.

"She might," I said. Either way, she'd saved us. No one was looking here anymore.

Syd and I left the dugout and went out to the field behind. We rolled over onto our backs and looked up at the stars while the grass grew cold beneath us. We talked about running and boys and our plans for summer and for the next school year.

Thanks to Ella, no one ever found us.

30.

now

Wait.

My mind is slotting some things into place.

What if I wish for someone, and then it turns out they were already back? Or had never vanished in the first place?

Because that 8/31 on the marquee?

I still swear that's new.

And what about the journal?

Someone else *could* still be here. They wouldn't have to work very hard to dodge me as I move around town. I haven't been playing this very smart. But that can change.

"Come on," I tell Yolo.

31.

now

Yolo and I pull into the parking lot at Lithia High.

There it is: The marquee says 8/31. I didn't make it up.

But it's changed again. There's more.

I slam on the brakes, stare up at the new words:

GET TH3M BACK.

That message.

The one that was in my journal.

Again.

My spine shivers in confirmation.

Because the date on the marquee—that *could* have been changed before everyone disappeared. It could have happened between the time I'd seen it yesterday morning and the time everyone vanished last night.

And someone could have found my journal, written in it, and left it in the woods before yesterday.

But *this*.

I know *this* is new.

Someone else is *here*.

32.

now

"I truly can't believe I wasted one of my wishes on you," I tell Yolo.

He glares at me.

Yolo and I are on a stakeout at the high school. We're sitting in the Subaru right in front of the marquee. We're ready. One of Jack's old baseball bats rests across my knees. We went back home to get it.

I stare up at the marquee.

GET TH3M BACK.

What do the words mean?

There are a few options.

Get them back, like I got Yolo back?

That's what I'm hoping. That's what I want.

GET TH3M BACK.

The words could also mean revenge. Like settling a score, an eye for an eye.

The time is coming around again. 8:31. When I think everyone disappeared.

If I wish, right now, something will happen. It has to.

I close my eyes.

I say a name in the dark.

33.

once

"Wait." Jack folded his arms and fake-frowned at me. "Sam's in *college?*"

"You don't get to have an opinion," I said. "You're my *little* brother."

He grabbed my phone and held it over his head. "Say that again."

"Ugh." Every time I called him my little brother, he did some variation of this. Grabbed my phone or my car keys or the bowl of cereal I was eating and held it up over his head, because I could no longer reach that high.

"Say it," Jack told me, "and you can have your phone back." Yolo twined himself around my legs as if he were on my side.

"Never," I told Jack.

My phone chimed with an incoming text. "Ooh," Jack said. "That's probably him."

I groaned. "Come on, Jack. Give it to me."

"I will if you say it."

"I'm not going to say it."

Another chime. Another text. Ugh.

"You can do it," Jack said. "Think about all the times you did this kind of thing to me when you were taller than I was. It's payback. It's only fair."

"Fine," I said, rolling my eyes. "You're my *big* brother."

"There you go." Jack handed me the phone. I glanced at the name on my screen.

Sydney.

Hey.

Can you come over?

Now?

I'd seen her that morning. We'd run together at practice, one of our best kinds of runs, both pushing the other to the limit where neither of us could speak, but where it also felt good. Legs matching stride for stride, adjusting pace to keep up with each other, taking turns pulling the other one along. The way we'd been running for years. Ella hadn't been able to keep up this time.

I felt a brief flash of irritation. Why did Syd think I was always at her beck and call? And why was it always on me to come over, to take us everywhere? Syd had a better car than I did, but she hardly ever drove anywhere. I wasn't really sure why.

Sam's on his way over. But later?

Her reply popped up a few seconds later.

Can you cancel?

She did this sometimes. Wanted me to prove that we were best friends, and that she came before anything or anyone else. But I'd promised Sam. And I'd been waiting all day for this. We were going to a concert on the university quad. I knew we'd stand there listening to the music and laughing and he would pull me close and wrap his arms around me from behind, electricity wherever our skin and bodies touched.

I wrote Syd back.

Is everything okay? Is it an emergency?

Sam pulled up to the curb out front. I could already feel his shoulders underneath my palms, his hips against mine. He opened the door and got out of the car, waving and grinning at me. A message buzzed again. I glanced down. Syd.

It's fine.

I put the phone in my back pocket and went to meet him.

34.

now

"We kind of suck at stakeouts," I tell Yolo, who is a paisley-shaped curl of warmth in my lap. I nudge him and he unfurls, yawning, kneading his too-sharp claws into my legs. It's morning, very early. Blue-pink light seeps over the sycamore trees that surround the school.

If the person I wished for came back, they didn't come at 8:31. Or for hours after that. Yolo and I both fell asleep at some point. Not for long, and not well, but I did close my eyes and drift somewhere.

Maybe it didn't work. When Yolo came back, it was immediate.

But Yolo wanted to see me. Maybe the person I wished for didn't want to be found.

Like whoever's been changing the marquee.

I keep coming back to that. There must be at least one other person here. Maybe two now.

"Well," I tell Yolo, "it's time to start breaking into things."

I heft the bat. We can smash the front door of the school, or a window. *Ooh*. The main office has those big windows along the back. For sure it's alarmed, but if it brings people running, all the better.

The door to the student government room where the

marquee letters are stored is metal, with a window in it too small to climb through, but I still have the key they gave me back when I was a class officer. So once I get into the school, it should be clear sailing.

I've got to figure out who else is here.

"You're going to want to stand back," I tell Yolo. He wanders away to a sunny patch of sidewalk, still keeping an eye on me. "Nice work," I say. "I think you're out of range." I raise the bat, thinking that I should probably be wearing goggles to smash windows. Shouldn't I? Oh well. I have a good swing, from practicing with Jack all those summers, and I know from that time he accidentally let his bat fly into our backyard window that the glass will mostly shatter in.

I assume my stance, imagine Jack is there to coach me. *Arm up. Back leg strong. Use your body.*

It takes me three tries to break the window. Yolo comes over to investigate, stepping gracefully.

"Hold on," I tell him. A few shards remain in the frame, jagged as icebergs. I take off my T-shirt and wrap it around my hand to break them away. Then I reach down for Yolo. He hates being picked up but lets me lift him and step inside. Then he's done, jumping out of my arms and hurrying deeper into the main office.

"This way," I tell him, pulling my T-shirt back on. But then, my eyes adjusting to the light inside, I realize something.

"You're a genius, Yolo," I say. *"Security cameras."* They've got to be in the main office somewhere, right? "I take it back. You are the best thing I could have wished for. I'm a lot smarter with you around."

Yolo gives a *meh* of agreement.

"Where do you think the footage is?" I ask. He's already sniffing behind the secretary's desk.

"It won't be there," I say. "Mrs. Collins is too normal."

As if he knows what I'm thinking, Yolo turns his head to look at the principal's office, its door standing open. It must have been left that way when the Vanishing/Rapture/Whatever occurred. The nameplate on the wall reads MR. WOLVERSON, PRINCIPAL.

Yolo and I step inside.

The principal's leather chair is tucked in at his desk. The blinds are closed. A Lithia High School football jersey hangs on the wall, as well as a picture of Principal Wolverson shaking hands with the mayor at the dedication of the remodeled auditorium two years ago. There's a candy dish on top of his desk, full of fun-size Milky Way bars. TV monitors hang on the wall facing the desk, and a bank of floor-to-ceiling cupboards lines the south wall. From within them come humming, electronic sounds.

I shudder.

"We're definitely in the right spot." Yolo cocks his head at me.

I've never been in here before, and it creeps me out. None of the female students like our principal. We call him "the Wolvermolester," and I get out of the way when I see his pot-belly and bald head swaying and shining down the hall. He always likes to hug the cross-country girls after a good race. The cheerleaders after a pep rally. The girls' basketball team after a game.

Men aren't supposed to be able to get away with that kind of thing anymore.

They usually do.

Of course his office is absolutely and certainly where all the security equipment would be.

"All right," I tell Yolo. "Into the breach."

35

Therapist: *I'd like you to close your eyes and imagine a safe place.*

What does it look like?

Sound like?

Feel like?

Is there anyone you would like to invite to your safe place?

Okay. I see that doesn't feel right to you yet.

That's all right.

It's okay for the answer to be no *or* not yet.

36.

now

"It's interesting that the Wolvermolester is so easy to hack," I tell Yolo.

Yolo doesn't seem to think it's all that interesting. He's standing in the doorway.

Principal Wolverton's username turned out to be his faculty ID handle, which I know from the emails he sends to the student body. It took me a few tries to guess his password, but when I typed in the mascot—hawks—plus the upcoming school year, I got it.

"Okay," I tell Yolo, clicking on a folder marked SECURITY and then on one marked FOOTAGE. Another click, and there's a folder marked with AUGUST of this year.

Yolo pads across the floor and hops up onto the desk next to me. I'm standing up, remote in hand. "The situation with technology all seems very arbitrary, Yo. Like how *this* stuff works fine, but I can't text anyone or get online."

Yolo cocks his head.

"Yeah," I say. "I guess it's not *that* arbitrary." The security system is internal, on a closed loop. But anything that might link me, physically or mentally, to the outside world at large (phones, internet, roads, the school alarm) doesn't work.

"Here we go," I say, and I click on the file.

37.

once

"Today's the day," Syd said.

"You don't have to jump, Ella," I said. "It's not even a Friday." It was a Tuesday night, dusky-gold.

"If you go now, it will be easier," Syd said. "The rest of the team isn't here."

"Other people are, though." Ella's eyes were wide.

"Not anyone you know," Syd said. "This will be good practice. Then you can do it again next Friday. You'll be the first freshman to make the jump."

"She looks scared," Sam said quietly to me.

"I know."

This hadn't been the plan. Ella wasn't supposed to be here at all. But that, I knew, was my fault.

Syd and I had seen Ella on the way to pick up Sam and Alex to hang out and, without thinking, I'd pulled over and asked if she wanted to come with us. She'd been hanging out in her yard, eating a Popsicle barefoot and watering her mom's flowers. Something about her tugged at me. I remembered being a freshman in high school and wanting in so badly. I couldn't drive past and wave and leave her there. After driving around for a while, we'd ended up at the jump somehow.

"All right," Syd said. "Who's going to go first, then? Show Ella how it's done?"

"I'll go," Alex said.

"Boring," Syd said. "You've done it a million times before. Sam, you do it. You've only jumped once."

"That *you* know about," Sam said, and he slid his hand around my waist. I leaned into him.

"Fine," Alex said. "I'll climb up into one of the trees and *then* jump." His dark eyes glimmered with mischief. "Will *that* be dangerous enough for you?"

"Hmmm." Syd drummed her fingers across her lips. "Let's see."

Ella made her way closer to the edge to look at the jump. Her back was skinny, shoulders so tense I could see every muscle through her thin cotton tank top.

I shouldn't have brought her. I hadn't realized how hard Syd was going to push her to jump.

But I thought I knew why.

Ella had beaten Syd at a workout for the first time a few days ago. She'd caught up with Syd and me with a mile to go. Syd had started to push the pace, relentless. I couldn't keep up with both of them, so I'd seen the finish from behind, Ella matching Syd stride for stride and then, at the end, pulling out ahead. When I got to the marquee, Coach was patting Ella on the back, and she was beaming at him, at me, at Syd, at everyone. Syd had said, "Nice run, Ella," and then told me later, "I had cramps. Stupid period."

But I wasn't so sure. I hadn't seen anyone give Syd that kind of serious competition in a long time. I never had.

And Ella was only a freshman.

Alex was making his way higher among the branches, his dark hair blending in with the tree, even as his bright blue T-shirt stood out like a piece of sky against it.

My heart pounded in my throat as he wriggled out along a branch that overhung the cliff, and I gripped Sam's hand tightly.

"You good?" I called up to Alex.

"Yeah."

"Geez," Sam said under his breath. "If he falls, he's going to break his neck."

Ella had made her way back over to us. Her face was pale.

Then Alex stopped climbing.

"I think he's stuck," Syd said. She was cracking up.

I heard Alex laughing.

"Hold on," he said. "I'm stuck."

"Called it," Syd said.

"Be careful," I hollered.

We heard some thrashing around in the trees. When I looked up, I saw Alex wriggling out of his T-shirt. He fell, laughing, all the way down into the water, his T-shirt staying there in the tree like a flag. A bunch of the college kids lying on the rocks below cheered.

When Alex had climbed back up to the top of the cliff, shining, his hair wet, I was furious. "Don't ever do that again. You could have gotten hurt."

"You going to climb back up and get your shirt?" Syd asked. "Jump out of the tree again?"

Why was she egging him on? Why was she egging *everyone* on?

"Are you kidding?" Alex widened his eyes in mock surprise. "I almost died once." He had his hands on his hips, his shorts sliding down just enough that I could see the band of his underwear, the spot where his tan line ended. "Nah. That shirt's old."

"Okay," Syd said. "You two next." She pointed at Sam and me.

"We should do a double jump," Sam said. "Here." He grabbed my hand. "On three. I'll count."

Our eyes locked. We each took a step closer to each other before we headed for the ledge.

Sam smelled like soap and grass and sweat and mint gum, and I wanted to touch the farm-boy, good-boy line of his jaw. So I did.

"Get a room," Syd said, but she was laughing.

Sam ignored her. He rested his hand against my back as we looked out at the jump. I could feel his fingers, warm. I wanted them on my skin and all over me, but we waited. We breathed, in. Out. He slid his hand down to hold mine, and we took a few steps away from the cliff to get momentum.

"One," he said. "Two. Three."

Together, we jumped.

As soon as we came up, spluttering, Syd splashed down next to us. She paddled over, hanging her tongue out like a dog, making me laugh in spite of myself.

"Ella's still at the top," Syd said.

I stopped laughing. "Crap," I said. "Be right back," I told Sam, who nodded, water still dripping from his hair. When he reached up to push it back, the line of his shoulders was so good that I wanted to swim right over and let him wrap me up in his arms the way he always did at night when we said goodbye.

But Ella was still up there, alone.

I swam over to the shore, pulling myself out of the water and heading for the path.

"You take your job as team captain wayyy too seriously," Syd said. To my surprise, she'd followed me out of the water and was right behind me. "I'm just messing around."

I spun around. "Stay here," I snapped. Syd stopped in her tracks, stunned. I never spoke to her like that. "Leave her alone. You'll make things worse." We stared at each other, both standing our ground.

"O-kay," Syd said after a second. She turned around and walked off, back toward the water. For a second, I wondered if I should go after her, but then I exhaled and headed for the top of the jump.

Ella was sitting on a fallen log to the side of the path a few feet away from the cliff. I might not have noticed her if it hadn't been for her candy-pink top visible through the trees. She looked up as I came toward her, twigs snapping under my feet.

"I can't do it," Ella said. She sounded like she might cry.

I sat down and put my arm around her. Her grasshopper shoulder blades, the warm skin of her back where her tank top didn't cover. "It's okay," I said. "You absolutely do not have to."

"Maybe could you come back sometime with me?" she asked. "Just us? And I could try again?"

"Of course," I said.

38.

now

The footage only goes back two days. No matter how hard I look, I can't find anything from earlier in the month—or from the last year, for that matter—on Wolverton's computer.

Weird.

"Where should we start?" I ask Yolo, my shaking fingers hovering over the mouse.

Yolo cranes his neck to see the screen.

"You're right," I say. "I should start at the beginning."

The morning of the day everyone disappeared. There's the cross-country team, meeting under the marquee.

I'm not there. I stopped going after last summer. I quit running my senior year.

I quit everything.

The teams scamper off on a run, they skitter back, they disband. I try not to look too closely at who is there. I try not to figure out from the amount of time it took which run they did.

I try not to think, *Are they carrying balled-up tank tops in their hands, is their hair wet, do they still go to Fall Creek even now?*

The day's footage speeds past before me.

There.

Yolo yowls at the exact moment I stop the tape.

"You see it, too, right?"

The screen fuzzes in and out, like in a horror movie, but someone is definitely there. At the marquee. Up on a ladder. The evening everyone disappeared.

Someone *did* change the message that day.

"I can't tell who it is," I tell Yolo, freezing the frame. "Can you?"

The image is somewhat distorted. It's hard to see the person's height, their distinct features. But the marquee itself is clear enough. I rewind and rewatch several times to make sure, but it's the same every time. Before, it says HAVE A GOOD SUMM3R. After, it says 8/31.

"Okay," I say. My heart feels like it's missing beats, and my hands are shaky. "Let's keep going, right?"

Yolo is on edge. His back is up, and I swear he's watching as closely as I am. He darts one quick glance at me before focusing back on the screen.

We move through the footage. Nothing happens until last night, when the marquee changed again, and the three words were added.

GET TH3M BACK.

The grainy black-and-white image distorts, skips. But I still see something. A ladder, propped up against the marquee. And then a blurry human figure climbing it. Again, I can't make out the details. But it is definitely a human being, with arms and legs and everything. *An actual person.* Someone else really is here. Because the footage of the person changing the marquee two days ago—that happened before everyone else disappeared. But this—this happened after.

"Holy crap," I say to Yolo, right as the image on the screen skips, sputters, disappears.

And that's it.

That's the end.

"No, no, *no*," I say, trying to move forward. I can't. There's no more footage. But.

Someone else is here.

"I'm not *totally* crazy," I tell Yolo.

I scroll back through the tape, go over the two times when the person is at the marquee. I watch them again, and again, and again.

"Is it the same person?" I ask Yolo. "Can you tell?"

Yolo's eyes don't leave the screen. The hair along his spine is standing up.

39.

once

Syd slid open the back window of the Alpha Kappa Sigma fraternity house. It was a hulking redbrick structure from the 1920s, perched at the edge of the Howell University campus along with all the other frat houses. She smiled wickedly over her shoulder.

"Something tells me this isn't the first time you've done this." Alex looked up at her, wearing a delighted grin he usually saved for me when I'd come up with an especially good idea.

Syd had texted me earlier that night. *Hang out with US for a change,* she'd written. *Me and Alex and Ella. Come on. I have an idea.*

The addition of Ella had surprised me. But I thought it was nice.

And I couldn't deny that I'd been spending a lot of time with Sam lately.

I already told Sam we'd hang out, I'd texted back. *Can I bring him?*

I expected nothing less, she'd texted back.

"I'll go in first," Sam said. "Make sure everything's okay."

"I've got it," Alex said, boosting himself up.

"Nice." Syd put her hands on her hips, tilted her head as if she were checking out his butt.

"I do my best," Alex said, struggling over the sill, and then we heard him *oof* as he hit the ground on the other side. "Hold on. Let me see if I can open a door." His shadowy figure moved away.

"How'd you find out about this place being open?" Ella asked, her voice low and excited.

"I heard my dad talking about it." Syd's father ran a construction company. They were renovating the fraternity house, hoping to have it back up and running before school started.

"You'd think they'd set up alarms at a site like this," Sam said.

"They usually do," Syd said. "But they had to turn them off because mice and raccoons kept triggering them. The security sign out front is just for show until they can get rid of the animals."

"Great," Sam said. "We're going to get rabies."

Syd laughed. "Are you afraid, college boy?"

The back door crept open. "All clear," Alex said. "Come on in."

Ella hesitated at the threshold. She wore a lavender T-shirt, cutoff shorts. The muscles in her legs were already changing, getting stronger, from running with us. And then she went through the door, Syd and me following.

"This way," Alex said, once we were all inside.

Scaffolding and plastic lined the walls and most of the windows, shifting in ghostly patterns as we moved through the building. The air was hot and close, and the floor was littered with plastic cups and mouse droppings.

Alex led us down the stairs, Syd right behind. Sam went after her, holding my hand, and I grabbed for Ella's. "Be careful," I warned her.

Linked, we came to the bottom of the stairs. Alex led us down the hallway, past a room that looked like a small kitchen, a bathroom, a laundry room, and into a long basement room. The carpet had been pulled up, revealing pockmarked concrete underneath. A couple of couches, a bunch of chairs, and some long wooden tables were stacked against the back wall. Two banners with Alpha Kappa Sigma's coat of arms emblazoned on them hung at the front of the room.

"This has to be the chapter room," Sam said. I hadn't dropped his hand, or Ella's.

"What's that?" she asked.

"It's where they do their meetings and have their secret ceremonies or whatever."

"The acoustics are creepy." I shivered in spite of the heat. "The whole room is creepy." With only the lights from our phones and everything shrouded, the entire place felt sinister.

I shot a glance over at Ella, feeling worried again about bringing her here. But she looked thrilled.

There were enormous pictures along the walls, propped up and covered in plastic. I knelt down to look more closely at them. The name of the fraternity—Alpha Kappa Sigma—then the name of the university, followed by the years the photos were taken. Rows and rows of guys wearing suits and ties. Faces looked back, teeth and hair and eyes bleary and blurred through the plastic.

"Do you think anyone's *died* down here?" Syd asked behind me. "Like, some kind of hazing thing gone wrong?"

"Could be," Alex said. "I feel like there are always stories going around about that. And they swear each other to secrecy or whatever."

"What exactly is our plan?" Sam asked. I could tell he wasn't as into this as the others were. He was about to start college. If he wanted to find out a fraternity's secrets, he could do that before too long.

But Syd and Alex and I were still more than a year away, and sometimes it felt like forever.

"We just want to look around," I said.

"Maybe have a ceremony," Syd said.

"Like what kind of ceremony?" Alex asked.

"We could summon a ghost," Ella suggested. We all turned to her in surprise. "Um, or not."

"That's a great idea," Syd said.

"I think we should probably sit in a circle," Alex said. "I don't know."

"We can use some of the chairs," Syd said, looking at the plastic-shrouded furniture. "Do you think there's, like, a fraternity throne or something?"

"Let's sit on the floor." Sam sounded very, very resigned.

"Relax, college boy," Syd said. "We're not going to ruin your chances of being a Big Brother in the frat of your choice someday."

We sat down on the floor in a circle and stared at each other.

"Um . . ." I began.

"Ah ooh wah ee a oh-oh-oh," Alex intoned.

I burst out laughing.

"You're doing *Finding Nemo*?!?"

Sam was laughing, too. He'd told me once that my laugh was contagious. I'd liked the compliment. I squeezed his hand again.

"Knock it off, you guys." Syd shook her head. "How are we supposed to summon anything if you're all acting like idiots?"

I tried to study her face in the light from our phones. There was an edge to her expression. Or was that the lighting, casting shadows and angles where they wouldn't normally be? Making her eyes more hollow and sad than they really were?

"What's going on, Syd?" I asked her quietly. So no one else could hear. "Is everything okay?"

She turned to fully look at me.

I still couldn't quite see her eyes. They were dark pools. Her face *was* sharper, though, I could tell now, which often happened during cross-country as we got leaner and leaner and in better shape as the season went on. But lately I thought that she'd been pushing it harder than ever to keep up with Ella.

Or was it something else?

It's this weird room, I thought, everything covered in plastic, where something bad had undoubtedly happened with that many guys living and drinking here over so many years.

Maybe no one had died here. But there are things that feel like death.

I knew Syd heard me. But she didn't answer.

"Okay," she said. "Let's summon someone. Anyone. We'll just put out a call. For whatever frat boy decides to show up."

"Bonus points if he's hot," Ella said, and Syd cracked up.

"Exactly, Ella," she said. "Here we go."

We closed our eyes.

40.

now

You'd think I'd know who I wished for. But the thing is
I can't be sure.

I may have said one name, but what if I wished for another
deep down in my heart?

It makes the most sense that it would be Syd. Right? The
cross-country team always met under the marquee before we
went out on our runs. It makes sense that she would leave me a
message there. That adds up.

Or Sam? I still dream about touching him. I still wake up and
ache that he's gone. That things went the way they did. That I'll
never again put my hand on his chest as he leans in to kiss me.

My heart is still racing. *Who is it?* Alex? We used to be in
student government together, in addition to cross-country. He
knows where to find the marquee letters. He was the person I
could always talk to, someone who really knew me. He knew
who I used to be and who I was at the end. Is he the one I want
here?

It could be my mom, my dad, Jack. But no. I love them,
they're my family, but would I *really* wish for them first?

Technically, I remind myself, *you wished for the cat first.*
Which makes me snort, and Yolo glances over.

But.

I remember the footage, what I saw at the marquee.

Maybe there are *two* people out here besides me.

The one I wished for, and the one I didn't.

41.

once

"Hey!" I called out to Syd and Alex. "I've got the food!" I held up a bag from Home Run Deli.

Alex and I are heading to Flatrock at noon, Syd had texted. *Maybe no Ella this time?*

I hadn't been bugged. We'd spent a lot of time with Ella lately. It was okay to still do our own thing sometimes.

Sure, I'd texted back.

Bring food, Syd had added. *Am feeling like Home Run. We'll get drinks.*

I didn't even have to ask what they wanted: Syd, turkey on white, no onions, add avocado. Alex, roast beef, extra cheese, no lettuce, on sourdough. I handed them each their sandwiches before sitting down on a rock near the edge of the river and taking out my own. I breathed in deep as I unwrapped my sandwich—club on wheat, easy mayo—and stuck my feet straight into the water, not bothering to unstrap my sandals.

"So no Sam?" Syd shielded her eyes to look at me. She was sitting right in the river in her bikini, her legs stretched out in front of her, her drink stuck in a shallow alcove to keep it cool.

"He's working." I didn't quite understand the slight edge I heard in her tone. Wasn't she glad I hadn't brought Sam for a change?

"I assumed you'd have him with you," Syd said. For some reason, she didn't sound pleased. I felt oddly out of place, like a third wheel, with her and Alex sitting next to each other and me on my own.

Alex slid a small cooler toward me. I leaned over to open it up. A couple of bottles of water, a Sprite, two Cokes, a cream soda. I took a water.

"So righteous," she said. "Coach would be proud."

We weren't technically supposed to drink soda—Coach hated it when we did—but most people broke that rule from time to time. Not me, not during the season. And Syd knew that.

But you *could* get kicked off the team for drinking alcohol.

I leaned back and took a huge bite of my sandwich, watching the kids splash around in the middle of the river, parents standing by. A toddler slipped, but her mother had her up again before the kid's butt even hit the water.

Flatrock was exactly what its name suggested. There was a spot at Fall Creek where the water got wide and the rocks were long, flat slabs. In the middle of the summer, the water ran just a few inches deep, perfect for wading, or for leaning back in and sunbathing. Lower down, there was a small spillway, nothing like the one out near the jump. This spillway was only a few feet high, and everyone used it like a slide. It was below us, and I could see kids getting into position at the top, ready to go down. A thin suspension bridge hung over the river below the spillway, barely visible from here. In the early mornings, mist came off the rocks and long-legged herons stood, dipping their beaks. Flatrock was at the first part of the Fall Creek run we did on Fridays, and I loved how different it looked on summer afternoons, strewn with people.

Syd stood up, reaching for her shorts near the edge of the bank. "I'm going down to the spillway."

"I'll be right there," Alex said. "Just going to finish this." He held up the last third of his sandwich.

"Take your time," Syd said. That edge in her voice again. She stepped into her shorts. I couldn't see her eyes behind her sunglasses, but I watched her walk away, sure-footed and smooth across the shallows of the river.

Alex finished his sandwich in two bites. "You eat like a wolf," I told him.

He rolled his eyes. "You tell me that every time I eat."

"You wolf every time you eat."

"I'm a growing boy."

I pretended to throw up, and Alex walked out into the river, laughing.

Something that only Alex and I knew was that we had once liked each other. *Liked* each other, as in boyfriend/girlfriend, as in we decided we should be together and see how it went. We didn't tell anyone because that way if it didn't work out, no big deal. We could go right back to being friends without any drama.

Which is exactly what happened. We went out for exactly two days and we kissed exactly one time, and it was kind of nice but we also burst out laughing right after. And I think during those two days we realized what we both had to lose, if we did do this for real.

And neither of us wanted that.

I ate my sandwich slowly and looked out at the dappled water, listening to the little kids, watching the tweens. Remembering how when I was a tween I wished I were me, a teenager with a car and friends at the creek. Now I was exactly all of those things.

Alex came plunging back through the water. "Thirsty," he said, and I raised my eyebrows. He laughed. "Not that way." He reached into the cooler, and I saw Syd waving me out to join her.

When I got to Syd, the two of us waded out farther, toward where the suspension bridge hung over the water. Her bikini top was emerald green. Mine was navy blue, and we were both wearing short running shorts over our bikini bottoms so we didn't get all scraped up going down the spillway. Everyone was looking. I mean, they started out looking at both of us, but it was her that their eyes stayed on.

In late August and early September, when the students came back, the college kids would claim Flatrock as their own, as if they'd discovered it. Frat boys would bring beers and whistle at us, acting like everything and everyone came into existence when they were here. What they never knew, what they couldn't even begin to understand, was that this was *our* town. They were, always, only visiting. If you don't live in a place the whole year long, it doesn't count as living. You're a visitor. You're temporary.

The students always swarmed into town in the fall like locusts. Some of them were rich and snotty and not sure how they felt about living in a town as small as Lithia when they were from New York City or Chicago or LA. Some of them had extremely entitled conversations with their parents in the aisles at Target, or acted like they thought it was ironic and hilarious to do Lithia things.

But they also had this energy about them. They were young and interesting and full of potential, and you hated them and wanted to be them at the same time. At least, I did.

"I love this place," I said.

"Yeah," Syd said. "It's pretty great." But her voice was flat, and she wasn't quite making eye contact. Why had she gestured for me to join her? Why had she asked me to come in the first place? What was going on?

"Hey," I said. "Syd. Should I go home? Seriously? I feel like I'm a third wheel without Sam. Like I'm kind of crashing a date." I waited for her to laugh, but she didn't.

She looked at me, her hazel eyes turned full-on green thanks to her top. "Nah," she said. "You're already here."

"Okay," I said, confused. It *wasn't* a date, right? Alex wasn't acting like it was. Plus, Syd and Alex? That wasn't a thing. That had never been a thing.

She waved her hand, but I was still on edge. Sometimes Syd did that. Acted like things were fine when they were clearly not.

"Seriously," I said. "What is it?"

"You've got Sam." Syd kicked her leg and the water splashed up, shimmered. "I should have someone, too."

"Alex?" I couldn't keep the surprise out of my voice. Syd had known Alex for years, and she'd never expressed interest in him before. She tended to go for guys who played football

or lacrosse and were tall and broad-shouldered, or who were in bands and had what she called "interesting damage."

Alex was cute and athletic in a rangy runner sort of way. He was interesting, but not very damaged.

"You sound skeptical," she said.

"I'm not," I protested. "Just surprised." And happy for Alex, I guessed. If he found out she was into him, he'd lose his mind. But *was* she really into him?

"Why?" Syd asked. "He's basically the guy version of you. And we hang out all the time." She was back to herself, that glint in her eye, her smile real again.

"That's true." I reached down into the water to pluck out a child-sized flip-flop that was floating past and tossed it to a mom nearby. "He and I *are* kind of the same person."

"Well, I can't date *you*." Syd reached up and pulled out the band in her ponytail, scooping her hair back again to make it tighter. "It would be like dating my sister."

I laughed. "Right."

"Whatever." Syd grabbed my hand. "Come on."

We went down the spillway screaming, the rush of water turning us slightly sideways as we slid. When we stood up, we started splashing each other, leaning into the water to swipe great swathes through it, shrieking with laughter.

"Everyone's staring," I said to Syd.

"Who cares." She smiled at me. Beads of water hung from her eyelashes, and her shoulders were golden in the sun. "Let them look."

42.

now

When I climb back into my car, I swear I smell watermelon lip gloss.

It's in my mind, I think. The sun's hitting the car and the interior is heating up, and when things get warm you can always smell them better, like when brownies are baking or you're stirring jam on the stove. Maybe the heat is making me smell something else, a square of bubble gum left in the back seat, an old air freshener shoved in a side pocket, and my mind is doing the rest, turning it into Syd.

Yolo yowls. He's not pleased about being carted everywhere with me, but I don't want to let him out of my sight.

"You're right," I say. "I mean, *you're* here."

Syd *could* be here. That *could* be her lip gloss I'm smelling.

Maybe I wished for her.

Or maybe she was already here.

Or. What if there *aren't* two people? What if I wished for someone who was already back?

The thought makes an almost-hysterical laugh bubble out.

That would be perfect. A total waste. It would be just like me.

I glance over at the glove compartment, where Syd used to put her apple stickers. I scraped most of them off last summer.

After. But they'd been there so long that they'd left a kind of gummy residue, and some hadn't peeled off entirely.

Wait.

There. On the glove compartment.

A fresh sticker, right in the middle.

I *know* that wasn't there before.

43.

once

Verity Ice Cream Flavors
Truly Delicious, Made with Real Cream

✓ **ALMOND COCONUT CRUNCH**—Coconut ice cream with chocolate chunks, toasted almonds, and coconut flakes.

✓ **BACON BOBBY**—Don't knock it till you've tried it! Bacon bits and bobs of maple nut in our creamy mocha ice cream.

✓ **BANANA BLITZ**—Like a banana split in a cone! Bananas, fudge, caramel, and maraschino cherries in our creamy vanilla ice cream.

✓ **BLACKBERRY (IN SEASON)**—Tastes exactly like summer! We source our berries from Taylor Farms.

✓ **BUBBLE GUM BLAST**—A childhood favorite for kids or kids at heart.

✓ **BUTTER PECAN**—Smooth, sweet, flavorful. You'll come back for it again and again.

✓ **CARAMEL CASHEW**—Rich and creamy, with our house-made caramel.

✓ **CHOCOLATE**—We don't mess with perfection. We've been serving this classic since we opened our doors in 1937.

✓ **CINNAMON CRUNCH**—Created by our founder's granddaughter in 1986, this favorite never goes off the menu!

✓ **COOKIE DOUGH**—Chocolate chip cookie dough from our founder's recipe, in our vanilla ice cream.

✓ FALL CREEK FUDGE—We don't skimp on the fudge, layering it in thick ribbons throughout our chocolate ice cream. This is a chocolate lover's dream!

✓ GORGE-OUS GREEN TEA—Our newest flavor, and already one of our most requested!

✓ HOWELL HONEYCOMB—Local honey and vanilla ice cream make this combination one that can't be beat.

✓ LITHIA LAVENDER LEMON—Spring and summer combined! Citrus and floral flavors in a perfectly purple ice cream.

✓ MAPLE—It's autumn all year long when you taste this! Maple syrup sourced locally.

✓ MARSHMALLOW MADNESS—House-made marshmallows in our chocolate ice cream.

✓ MINT CHOCOLATE CHIP—A favorite for decades, with the perfect ratio of mint and chocolate.

✓ MOCHA—Coffee and cream the way you like it.

✓ MUDSLIDE—We load it in! Chocolate ice cream, espresso flavoring, peanuts, marshmallows, and pretzels.

✓ OREO—Cookies-and-cream perfection.

PEACHES AND CREAM (IN SEASON)—Fresh peaches, never frozen, from local farms.

RASPBERRY (IN SEASON)—Pucker up! Our raspberries are sourced from Taylor Farms.

STRAWBERRY (IN SEASON)—You'll feel like you're at the farmers' market on a Saturday morning.

VERITY VANILLA—It's a classic for a reason! Creamy perfection, our original recipe.

44.

now

I should have come here right after I went to Alex's. I've been avoiding it, which is stupid.

Sydney's parents have more money than mine, and their house shows it. It's shingled in gray and painted with white trim, and the shutters are red. Tastefully clipped boxwoods line the drive, and the trees out front are old, substantial. It's the kind of rich and discreet home you could never build nowadays, full of the charm and taste that a place earns over the course of years. There's a perfectly rendered addition at the rear of the home that Syd's dad built when they moved to Lithia the summer before our sophomore year. It probably cost as much as my entire house. I worry I'm going to have to shatter one of their windows to get inside.

But when I round the corner, it turns out that when the Rapture or the Vanishing or Whatever happened, Sydney's family had left a kitchen window wide open.

Weird. If there's one thing Mr. Thompson doesn't like, it's wasting money on having the air-conditioning running when there's a window open.

Or. Maybe Syd opened it when she came back. This morning, when it was cool. Maybe she's out for a run, right now. If I left, went on one of our old routes, would I find her? Could I catch her?

THE ONLY GIRL IN TOWN

Better to stay here, for when she comes back. I shoulder my way through the window, clambering across the kitchen counter and dropping ungracefully to the floor. Behind me, Yolo jumps easily inside and trots along the counter.

"Show-off," I say, as he springs from the counter to the kitchen table, as if he's playing that game we used to play when we were kids when we tried to not touch the ground and crawled across the furniture. *Hot lava.* When someone made a mistake and touched the hardwood or the carpet, there was a tiny thrill that ran through me, wondering if they'd really get burned, even though I knew none of it was real.

Alex would have understood my going into his house.

But I'm one thousand percent sure Sydney would be pissed about my being here.

"You want to know what we're looking for?" I ask Yolo.

He does not. He wants to wander off in the direction of the living room, which has several very plump and cushy couches available for his use.

I climb the stairs to the second story, walking along the vintage runners on the hardwood floors, passing their family pictures on the wall. Here they are one Christmas, wearing thick cable-knit sweaters. And at the beach, a tween-aged Syd standing between Mr. and Mrs. Thompson while a perfect summer day—sand, blue sky, puffy white clouds—rolls out behind them. Syd was so pretty, so blond and beautiful, even as a kid, and her parents were tall and slender and golden. I know this is a curated gallery, but still. Not many families could aspire to a set of photos like this.

When I get to Syd's room, I stop in my tracks in the doorway, not anticipating how much of a gut-punch I'd feel being here again. Tears start to my eyes, but I brush them away. No time for that.

I don't know what I'm wishing for, what I'm expecting. A journal with *WHY I DON'T LIKE JULY ANYMORE* written across the cover? Or *WHAT REALLY HAPPENED?*

Her bed's made, which is weird. It's like the way Jack's chair was tucked in after he vanished. Syd *never* made her bed. It was always a tangle, her comforter and sheets twisted up from the way she threw them aside dramatically when she got out of bed every morning. It made me laugh when she did that, and she always looked at me, bewildered, because she did it unconsciously, as if she were mad at the world for catching her lying down and she was hoping to throw it off the scent by hurtling out of bed.

I take a step into her room. For a moment, I pull up short in a panic, thinking there's someone here, but it's only me, in the mirror. The one with the bulletin-board frame. I walk closer, avoiding my own eyes.

There's no pictures of me on the board. There used to be one, right here. It was of the two of us after the state meet our sophomore year, arms slung around each other's shoulders, matching blue-and-gold uniforms. We'd braided our hair the same, a complicated kind of crown braid that neither of us could do on ourselves but could manage just fine on the other. Strands of both our braids had escaped and were blowing across our faces. We were squinting into the sun; I was laughing, she was smiling. One of my hands had come up to my cheek to push away the strands. We each had a temporary tattoo of a butterfly high on our right cheekbones, put on for good luck before the race.

When Syd moved here, she was so golden and beautiful and interesting and athletic that everyone who met her wanted her. The cheerleaders tried to talk her into trying out for cheer that winter. The soccer coach wanted her for his team.

But we already had her. "I can't believe our luck," Coach said, because she was exactly what our team needed, with so many seniors graduating. She was fast and unafraid and stubborn.

I couldn't believe *my* luck. To have her as my best friend.

I open the closet.

I know some of her clothes, but not all of them. The gray sweatshirt hoodie with the orange stripe across the chest, I remember from fall our sophomore year. She wore it all the time, so often that the cuffs are frayed. The white eyelet top she wore to my birthday party one year. The skirt that she wore to the Homecoming game junior year.

I don't know why it turned. Why we started getting jealous of each other, in weird ways. I don't know what I did, but it must have been something. Or maybe it was nothing and we had to turn it into something to make it end, to make it easier.

But what? Why?

I turn away from the closet.

There's her phone, right on the nightstand. She would never have left it behind. I pick it up. I try to power it on, but it doesn't work. Dead battery? I rifle through the drawers, pull out a charger, try a few different outlets.

Nothing. The phone won't turn on. I can't find anything out that way.

So instead, I go back to the closet.

I pull a navy-blue top off the hanger. I've never seen it before. She must have bought it recently. The tags are still on. I used to know every piece of her clothing, and she knew mine. We swapped sometimes. But not anymore.

When did you get that shirt?

When did you cut your hair?

When did things start to change between us?

When did we decide to leave each other behind?

And then I hear a door slam below.

45.

once

"Nice run," Syd said to Ella, exhaustion and admiration mingled in her voice. The two of them had been fast the whole run, and for the last quarter mile they'd been outright racing, long legs matching long legs, stride for stride for stride.

I hadn't been able to keep up with them at the very end, but I hadn't been that far behind. Close enough to tell that it had been pretty much a dead tie when they reached the spot near the marquee that marked the unofficial start and finish of every run.

"Let's get out of here before the rest of the girls catch up," Syd said, already heading for my car. "I'm starving. Ella, you want to come get breakfast with us?"

"Um, yeah," Ella said, beaming. "That would be great."

As we drove the few blocks to Zippy's Diner, Syd turned back to look at Ella. "That was insane. You're going to make sure I run the fastest time in the state this year, aren't you?"

"Sure," Ella said, easy as that, and Syd laughed.

She'd fully accepted Ella.

Hadn't she?

Was I glad?

Syd and I had done this—gone to breakfast at the diner after practice every now and then—ever since we were sophomores, back when we didn't have cars and our parents had to drop us off and we were supposed to walk home or find rides with the upperclassmen.

Back then, we had no jobs, no responsibilities. We would walk to Zippy's and eat all we wanted and horse around downtown before we wandered home or texted someone to come and get us.

"They change the fruit in the pancakes depending on what's in season," I explained to Ella as we sat down at a table. My fingers stuck to the menu. Everything at Zippy's was always a bit sticky.

"I know," Ella said. "I've been here before."

"Right," I said. I shouldn't have assumed. Just because a place felt so like it was Syd's and mine didn't mean other people didn't know it.

The waitress, Colleen, stood over us, order pad already in hand. "Don't tell me. You want the pancakes. Full stack."

"Yes, please," I said.

"Same," Syd added.

"Me too," Ella said.

Colleen sighed dramatically. "You girls outeat the Howell men's hockey team," she called over her shoulder as she walked away.

She told us that every time.

"Look." Syd slapped down a small, green cloth-covered book on the table. An actual puff of dust rose up from it. "Look what I got."

"Where on earth did that come from?" I asked.

"I put it in your glove compartment this morning when I got in the car," Syd said. "I thought you saw me."

"No, I mean originally," I said. Something about it looked familiar. The coat of arms embossed on the cover, the Greek letters on the front . . .

"I took it from the chapter room at Alpha Kappa Sigma," Syd said. "Don't worry, I'll take it back. Plus, I think Carl wanted us to find it."

That cracked me up in spite of myself for a second. Carl was the name of the ghost we'd "summoned" when we'd broken into the fraternity house. Syd had given him a name, and we'd all come up with a backstory that was so ridiculous that even Sam had been adding to it by the end of the night.

"What is it?" Ella asked.

"It's their secret book. With, like, their secret rules. They give it to the new pledges."

I glanced around the diner. During the school year, lots of college guys, especially athletes, ate here. And some of them might be in town for summer training. "What if someone here is in that frat?"

"July," Syd said, laughing. "Don't be so paranoid."

"I'm not paranoid," I said. "Don't you watch any movies? Haven't you heard the stories?"

"Some of the stuff in here is hilarious," Syd said. "It's like, old-school. They have a chart that tells you how to set a formal table. There's a whole section about manners."

Ella had taken the book from Syd, was turning its pages.

"There *is* some secret-society stuff," Syd said. "Secret signs. Ceremonies. But it's pretty dorky."

"And there's a note at the front about how if you lose the book you're going to die," Ella added.

"That's just posturing," Syd said.

"You should take it back," I said.

"We need to make something like this for the team," Syd said.

"We're not making a creepy frat book for the team."

Syd took the book from Ella and leaned forward in her seat, flipping through the pages. "Not a whole book," she said. "Only this part." She'd landed on something. I peeked over but couldn't see. Her eyes were intent on whatever the print on the page spelled out, her fingers tan against the green cloth cover. "A manifesto."

46.

now

It could be the wind that slammed that door.

It's not. I know it's not.

I race down the hall, the perfectly polished length of hardwood, and turn so hard into the stairwell that I slip, catch, almost fall. I right myself and thunder down the stairs, not caring who's heard, Yolo in quicksilver black-cat pursuit.

I throw open Syd's front door. The grass is heavy with water, and I glance down hoping for tracks, for a sign that someone besides me was here.

I sprint to the street and look up and down. I can't see anyone.

I jump in the car, Yolo right behind me.

Which way to go?

Left, or right?

I don't want to lose them.

47.

once

SAM
Hey

JULY
hey

SAM
what's up

JULY
not much

Working on this manifesto thing
for the team

SAM
A what?

JULY
Like a mission statement, maybe?
A creed? I don't know.

SAM
Let me guess. Syd talked you into it

JULY
sort of

I also kind of volunteered because
I didn't want it to get too weird. It
started out as an oath but now
we're calling it a manifesto

SAM
Got it

SAM

Also I know I saw you earlier tonight but I already want to talk to you again 😄

JULY

call me if you want

or we can just text

whatever

SAM

Okay

Maybe text

This way I can think about what to say to you before I say it

JULY

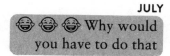 😂 😂 😂 Why would you have to do that

SAM

You're kind of intimidating

see

That's the kind of thing I want to say but haven't dared say to your face

JULY

What?!?

You think I'm intimidating? 😂

SAM

um, yes

JULY

I think you're thinking of Syd

SAM

see, that's the thing

I'm not

SAM

Why do you always say that, anyway?

JULY

She's usually the one people notice.
No guy has ever gone for me
over her before

SAM

No way is that true

JULY

fact

SAM

Alex didn't

JULY

Um wrong again

SAM

he's wanted to be with you for a long
time. I can tell

JULY

nope

SAM

yup

It's so obvious

But I don't want to talk about
Syd and Alex

I want to talk about you

JULY

that feels awkward

SAM

okay I'll stop soon. But first I want to
say how gorgeous and smart and fun
you are

there

SAM

I'm done

actually you can keep going

SAM

Oh good

I will

48.

now

I decide to turn right, into town, winding down the roads, taking the curves faster than I should.

I won't give up. I can't.

I will find whoever else is here.

I drive for hours, Yolo yowling and then sleeping in the back seat. I try to catch someone around a corner, glimpse a light in a window coming on. I take the turns so sharply that something rolls around in the trunk, annoyingly, but I have no time to stop and see what it is.

49.

once

I took a deep breath of satisfaction, looking down at the rows of bushes, at the low green hills outlined by a smudge of blue where they met the sky. Humidity and bees hovered in the air. The closer you got to the bushes, the more you realized how many raspberries there were, clustered like bright red gems.

"Look," I told Drew, Annie, and Kate, who were gathered around, holding tight to the rinsed-out plastic ice cream tubs I'd brought with me from home. We used them every year for berry picking. Coming to Taylor Farms was part of my ongoing plan to make sure the Miller kids had a perfect Lithia summer.

I knelt down in the dirt and pushed apart the leaves to reveal a cluster of raspberries. "When they're ripe, they almost drop off into your hand." I popped one into my mouth.

"Isn't that stealing?" Drew asked. He was always very worried about the rules.

I smiled at him. "We won't eat very many. And I'll tell them to add a little to the total at the end when we weigh them."

That satisfied him. He glanced over at where the farmers sat in the shade of a small tent, a scale and a cash box between them. One of the women waved at him, and he ducked his head.

We started making our way along the row. I heard Annie

humming to herself as she picked. It was impossible to imagine
that it would ever be winter. The sun was starting to lower, everything turning gold and green, so rich I felt like I could reach out
and pluck the landscape the way I'd picked the raspberries. I could
hold a tree in my hand. I could run a cloud between my fingers.

"When we're done, we'll bring the berries home and eat
them with cream," I told the kids. "And we can make jam out
of them."

"You really know how to make jam?" Annie asked, and I
laughed outright at the awe in her voice.

"It's not hard," I said. "We'll make it tomorrow."

My phone rang. Syd. I took a step or two away from the
kids and answered, my eyes still on them, their hands, the tops
of their heads.

"July," she said, without preamble. "It's perfect."

I knew right away what she was talking about. I'd finished
writing the manifesto for the team the night before and texted
it to her. When Syd had big ideas, she often wanted me to help
execute them.

"You don't have to say that. We can change it if you want."

"You know I wouldn't say it if I didn't mean it."

I did know that.

"That's great." I shielded my eyes, made sure I could see all
three kids as they kept making their way down the row. They
were intent on their buckets, their berries.

"That first line especially is killer," Syd said.

"Thanks." I had to admit, I'd been proud of that one in particular.

"And I loved the title," Syd said. "'The Fall Creek Girls Manifesto.'"

"Yeah, I was wondering what you'd think about that," I said. "I started out calling it 'The Lithia High School Girls' Cross-Country Team Manifesto,' but that seemed really long. And then when I thought of this, it seemed right. Kind of like it goes on past high school. We're teammates for life."

"Exactly," Syd said. "I'm telling you, it's perfect. I already went ahead and printed out copies. We can give them to everyone on the team."

"Wow, okay."

"I printed them on this really fancy paper," Syd said. "They look old-fashioned. Kind of epic. Wait until you see them. We're the best team captains ever."

"Legends," I agreed.

"When do you think Ella will jump?"

"We shouldn't push her," I said, watching Drew place another berry in the bucket. He was so careful.

"I think she'll be ready soon," Syd said. "She's tougher than you think."

I wasn't so sure about that. Every time we were at the jump, I could see the fear in Ella's eyes.

Annie had come up close to me. She tucked her hand in mine. "I think I'm done," she said. Kate was making her way toward us down the row.

The smell was earth and moisture, lush growth from generous decay. The sun hit Annie's hair and caught its red and gold strands. I thought about the old book *Blueberries for Sal*, and

wondered if I should read it to Annie later, or if it would make
her scared of bears.

But she didn't have to be.

There were no bears.

We were so, so safe.

50.

now

Finally, at a loss for what else to do, I drive back to Syd's house and park my car out front, staring up at her windows. Is she here? Did she go back inside?

How am I ever going to do this, if they don't want to be found?

But what if Syd—or whoever it is—isn't going along the road?

What if they're literally going cross-country? Through yards, over fences, hiding, waiting?

There's no way one person can look everywhere in an empty town. Even in a single empty house earlier, she gave me the slip.

I slump back in my seat.

Yolo climbs into my lap.

"You're right," I say. "I guess we should go home." I turn the key in the ignition, and start driving, just a bit too fast. But I want to crawl under the vanity and hide, go to ground.

And then I realize.

That rolling sound.

That happens when I take the turns too sharp.

That wasn't there yesterday.

I screech to a stop.

Run around to the back of my car.

And open the trunk.

51.

once

How's camping going? Sam texted.

I'm having the time of my life, I wrote back. *Remind me again why you and your family love to do this.*

"Phone, please," my mom said, holding out her hand.

I looked over at Jack for backup.

"She already took mine," he said. "And Dad's."

"None of us are going to use our phones for the next twenty-four hours." My mom put them all in her backpack's inner pocket and made a big show of zipping it up. When she was finished, she patted the bag. "I'll sleep on this if I have to."

"Um," my dad said. "I kind of need to check on some work stuff."

"Sam's going to think I broke up with him," I complained.

"My friends are going to think I died," Jack huffed.

"Fine." Mom rolled her eyes so hard her ponytail bounced. She was wearing a tank top and leggings. With her hair pulled up, she looked like a girl from a distance, like one of my friends. "Twelve hours. We can all do twelve hours, right? Besides, we're all right here. Who else could we need?"

My mom was in what we called Vacation Mode. She was alternately kind of the best (a ball of adorable, happy energy) and the worst (having big ideas like taking away our phones). She'd booked a campsite at Hopkins Glen State Park for the weekend, and it was obvious from the moment she'd told us about the trip that we were in for it.

"We're getting away to nature," she said. "It's been so long."

"The last time we got away to nature in this particular state park, Jack threw up in my mouth," I said.

"I was four," Jack said. "It's not like I had any control over where I barfed."

"We're too old for this," I said.

I thought I heard my dad mutter *"So am I"* under his breath, but when I looked over at him, he was still methodically tending the fire.

"You two," my mom said. "Come help me make the tinfoil dinners."

Jack and I groaned in unison. She knew how to get to us. We were both absolute suckers for tinfoil dinners. Also s'mores. Also Dutch oven peach cobbler, which my dad was the best at making. Everything tasted so good outside.

But that night, as bugs thudded against the zipped-open tent skylight, and as the humidity lay over us like a blanket your parents put on you that you hadn't ever wanted in the first place, I couldn't keep from complaining again. It was hot and muggy and Jack smelled like teenage boy.

"Why are we even doing this," I said.

"To save money," Jack said, on the other side of my tent. Which was not far enough away.

"We can hear you," my mom said, from the tent she and my dad were sharing. "You know it's not about the money."

"Oh, isn't it," Jack said darkly.

"We're doing this to bond," my dad said. "And to experience nature."

"This is the only time we could go, with all of your schedules." My mom sounded wistful. "Remember when we used to go on vacation for a whole week?"

"Those were the days," Jack said.

"The days when you barfed in my mouth," I said.

"It is nice to have July with us," Jack said. "She's been *very busy* this summer."

"So have you," I said.

"Not the same," Jack said. His voice had an edge. "You're gone *all* the time."

"That's not true."

"It's been all Sam, all the time," Jack said. "The Summer of Sam."

That made me laugh. "That sounds like a horror movie."

"Oh, trust me, it is," Jack said.

"All right, all right," my dad said. "Get some sleep."

"I would, if I weren't scared of Sam crashing through the forest to find us," Jack said. "'July! July! Where are you?'"

"This is how dating someone works," I said. "Which you would know, if you ever dated anyone."

"Hey," Jack said. "I had a girlfriend last spring."

"For about five minutes."

"Enough, July," my dad said. "You need to get some sleep, too."

"I would, if all these bugs would shut up," I said. As if to prove my point, the cicadas screaming in the trees seemed to raise their pitch.

"You'll feel better in the morning," my mom said.

"I'd feel better if I had a camping cot," I said. "Like you and Dad."

"Tell you what," Dad said. "You work hard and support your family the way your mom and I do, and then you can buy yourselves cots, and then it will be your turn to lie in your own tent and feel really comfortable while your ungrateful kids whine at you."

"I love you, Dad," Jack said. "I love you, Mom."

"Stop kissing up to them," I said.

"I love you, July," Jack said. I could tell he was grinning when he said it. "*So* much."

"Ugh," I said. "Stop it." But I was smiling, too.

I don't remember falling asleep, but I remember waking up in the middle of the night.

I was lying flat on my back, staring up at the tent, my camping pad not doing much to cushion me against the stones on the ground. A bug thudded against the side of the tent near my face, and I knew that eventually I was going to have to find a flashlight and stagger alone through the dark to a disgusting campground porta-potty. I shouldn't have had so much lemonade with my tinfoil dinner.

Everyone else was asleep.

I looked up through the skylight at the stars.

I had the feeling again for a moment. The one I'd been trying to push away since I was eight. The cold lonely.

I kept staring at the stars. My back was on the dirt, where I would someday go again.

But I'm here now, I thought.

Aren't I?

52.

now

It's a baseball.

There, in the back, with the things that my dad has us keep on hand in the trunks of any cars we own: a first aid kit, bottled water, granola bars, a blanket. This one is blue-and-red plaid, a quilt my grandma made before she died.

I don't think the baseball was here before I heard the door slam at Syd's house. I would have noticed, right?

But why would Syd leave me a baseball?

Wait.

Think think think.

At first nothing comes to me, but then in a flash it does.

That night on the fields. Playing hide and seek.

"A little on the nose, Syd," I say.

But is it Syd?

"So you're playing hide and seek again now? Okay. I'll play this your way. I'll keep following the clues."

My voice is confident, assured. As if I know for sure it's Syd. As if I don't have a doubt in the world about who is here with me and where I'm going next.

But I have so many questions.

Who are *you?*

What happens next?
Where
does this end?

53.

once

"I wish my roommate was out of town every weekend," Sam said. We were sitting in his tiny dorm room, our knees practically bumping, my back against his roommate's bed, Sam's back against his. The desk chairs were too uncomfortable to sit in.

"Luxurious," I agreed.

Sam laughed. "There's a reason I like hanging out away from the dorms."

Secretly, though, I loved it. This was the part of Howell that we townies never got to see. We ran through its campus, sure, and went to concerts on its quad. But the inner sanctums, places like the old stone dorms, with their diamond-paned glass—I'd never been in one before. Even with the blond-wood furniture and the industrial-strength carpet, I felt like history was soaking into me. Like it could be a hundred years ago somewhere outside that window. Water running through the gorges like it had for centuries. Before anyone even thought of the school, the town.

"Switch?" I asked, and Sam handed me his orange chicken in its container, and I handed him my broccoli beef. We were eating Chinese takeout we'd picked up from a restaurant in Collegetown, the neighborhood nearest the campus. Walking back through Howell together, past the clock tower, I felt like I was coming into my own. Like I was crossing over into worlds that had always been here but could finally be mine.

"You're the only girl I've ever met who can outeat me," Sam said.

"I know you think it's hot," I told him, stabbing my fork through another piece of orange chicken. We'd run eight miles that morning, and I'd been hungry all day.

"I do, actually," he said. He grinned at me. "Everything about you is hot."

"Good," I said. "And ditto." I bumped his knee with mine.

I was about to crumple up the bag when I remembered something.

"Ooh," I said. "I almost forgot about the fortune cookies." I reached inside and took out the two plastic-wrapped cookies, tossing one to Sam.

He caught it single-handed, setting his takeout container on the floor with the other hand. "Same time," he said, and we both unwrapped our cookies, snapping them in half to reveal the slips of paper inside. Sam slid his out and held it up. "Mine says, 'Great things are ahead for you.'"

"Mine's blank."

He laughed. "No way. You're making that up."

"I'm not."

"Let me see."

I handed him the paper slip. Our fingers touched.

"Huh," he said, staring down at it. "I've never seen that happen before."

"Me neither." It was hot. I lifted my hair from my neck, wishing I had a ponytail holder.

"The air-conditioning in this place is crap," Sam said. "Here." He stood up and went to the window to open it. The air that came in wasn't much cooler than inside, but it had motion to it, and smelled like summer. I got up so that I could look out, too. Sam's room was on the top floor of the dorm, so I could see all the way to the gorge that cut through campus, the rock and water in shadows at this time of dusk. I could see the town sparkling in the distance, past the summer-green of old trees waving at us. The stars were coming. The bell in the Howell University clock tower tolled, eight times.

I felt a kind of deep satisfaction, a sense of arrival. A *here I am, on the inside of a place that has kept me out.*

It wasn't like my parents could afford a place like Howell. Even if I decided to try and get in. If you're inside these dorms, that means you made it. You just have to hang in there and not throw yourself into one of the gorges. Every year, a couple of desperate students did that, usually during winter when the gray began to get to them.

I tucked the slip of fortune paper into my bra, and Sam raised his eyebrows. "What?" I asked. "I don't want to lose it." The running shorts I was wearing didn't have pockets.

I'd decided that the blank fortune meant good luck. That I could write whatever I wanted on it.

Sam wrapped his arms around me from behind and I leaned into him.

So many ways to fall in this town.

54.

—*Written on a blank fortune cookie slip in July Fielding's handwriting.*

55.

now

This has to be the right spot.

I'm sitting in the baseball dugout, where Syd and I hid that night when Ella went out and took the fall for us. I left Yolo curled up asleep in the back seat of the car, a window cracked for air.

The only thing in the dugout is a red-painted bench, flakes of the paint coming away in shards and splinters.

It's getting dusky, but I can still see well enough to know that there's nothing in here besides the bench, the dirt on the ground, the tramped-down bits of litter. I've run them through my fingers. I even crawled under the bench and looked up to see if there was anything taped there or left underneath. Just chewed gum, a variety of colors and shapes that looked strangely beautiful in the evening light.

So I've got dirty hands and dirty hair.

But no clue. No idea of where to go. I lean back for a moment, tired, my head against the concrete wall of the dugout. I close my eyes, remembering how it felt that night, to be in here. With other people. With Syd, and Ella.

I breathe in deep.

56.

Mom
Dad
Jack
Sydney
Sam
Alex
Ella
yolo

—List written on a hot-pink Post-it in July Fielding's handwriting.

57.

now

I'm hoping to catch another whiff of watermelon lip gloss, of something that makes me think of Syd or someone else.

But there's only the smell of cut grass and dirt and old wood.

It reminds me of that night, of course, but there's nothing new.

Wait.

Is there?

Another deep breath.

And then I smell it.

Fresh spray paint.

Close by.

But where?

I don't see it until I walk around to the back.

There, bright red against the yellow-painted cement of the dugout.

GET TH3M BACK.

58.

once

"Who's winning?" I asked Alex. We were almost at the end of the course. We had three holes left. Mount Rushmore, Redwood, Yellowstone.

"I am," he said. "As always."

"It's just because I always let you," I said.

"Ha." Alec putted toward Theodore Roosevelt, who was missing his nose. He sank it. "I'm unstoppable now that I have this," he said, twirling one of the golf clubs I'd given him as a gift. "Who knew they even made miniature golf club sets? I thought everything was putters."

"It took some sleuthing," I said. "I may have had to drive to Cortland to meet a guy in a shed who's a metalworker."

"Good grief," Alex said. "That sounds dangerous."

"It wasn't," I said. "He was legit. And like eighty years old." I rolled my shoulders. "What's the actual score?"

Alex scratched at the tiny notepad he was carrying. "Huh," he said. "We're tied."

"Hmmm," I said. "That's surprising."

I putted. It went right into the face of the one of the dudes in Mount Rushmore—Washington—and then bounced into the hole perfectly.

"Come *on*," Alex said.

I did finger guns. A victory dance. "Please," Alex said. "Make it stop."

I did not make it stop because: I was on fire. "Where do you want to go to lunch? If this keeps up, I'm buying."

"Will Sam be cool with that?"

"Why wouldn't he be?" I looked at Alex to make sure he was being serious. He was.

Alex shrugged. "Just asking."

I scooped up my ball and we headed for the redwoods.

Alex lined up his ball and lifted his club to putt. I whacked him on the butt with my golf club as he bent over. "Get it."

"You're the worst," he said, lining up again, and then he said, "I'm going to hit this before you can mess me up again," and he sliced away at the ball, and it went right up the ramp and perfectly into the hole in the trunk of the largest redwood tree.

Alex hoisted his club over his head in victory. "Look at that."

"Preettty nice," I said. "But too bad you didn't get this on Yellowstone. No free game for you."

"It's like the whole thing with the tree falling in the forest and no one there to hear it," he said, mock distraught. "If I get a hole in one anywhere besides Yellowstone, does it count at all?"

"It does," I said. "I saw it."

59.

now

This stupid message again.

GET TH3M BACK.

And they didn't *have* to write a three this time. That was only necessary for the marquee because we didn't have enough Es. They didn't use the three when they wrote in my journal.

But now here it is again.

So is it a clue?

Are there three people I have to get back?

Or is it the three wishes thing?

And where am I supposed to go from here?

Suddenly, I'm livid.

Who's here? Why are they leading me?

Why are they *leaving* me?

"You're going to have to do better than this," I holler. "I'm going home." I stalk my way back across the field toward my car.

When I get there, I pause, looking across the asphalt and grass and trees as the sun sets.

I climb inside my car and slam the door as hard as I can.

60.

now

I haven't even turned the key in the ignition before I realize something's wrong, and almost immediately I know what it is.

Yolo's not in the car.

61.

now

How did he get out?

I left the window open a crack so he would have fresh air, but it's not wide enough for him to get through. Is it?

I walk through the field. Check the dugout. Come back to the car. He's still not here.

I drive slowly, slowly, looking for the flash of his eyes all along the road.

Nothing.

Cats can find their way home. Can't they? Haven't I read that somewhere? And Yolo's smart. He might be home by now.

I pull up in front and race for the door, calling out as I go inside. I look by the cat door into the garage, check every room, under every bed, behind every piece of furniture.

"Hey, Yolo," I call out. "You hungry?"

I pour his cat food into a bowl. Usually that sound brings him running from any corner of the house.

"Yolo?" My voice shakes.

Maybe he's mad about what I said.

He can't be lost.

"I did mean to wish for you," I say. "I did. I did. I'm so glad you're back. Yolo, please come back."

62.

now

He's upstairs, in the bathroom where I sleep, curled up in the spot under the vanity. I didn't see him the first time I came through because he was so tucked in.

"Yolo," I say, and the tears almost almost come, but they are stuck.

"You freaked me out," I say. "You're so smart. So smart. You made it all the way home."

I don't know how he got out of the car or into the house, but I do know this: I'm never letting him out of my sight again.

63.

once

"You really don't have to give me this," I told Sam. In my hands I held the small brown-paper box he'd handed me, tied with a red ribbon. "It's not actually my birthday."

Jack was laughing outright. "Oh man," he said. "It's happening *again*."

"Wait," Sam said. "What?"

The three of us were sitting in lawn chairs in the backyard. We'd submerged our feet in the plastic kiddie pool that my mom kept around for super-muggy summer days like this. Every now and then our feet brushed against each other's in the water. The air still smelled like hamburgers. Or maybe someone else nearby was grilling late. My parents had gone inside to get dessert ready, and if I turned my head slightly, I could see them in the well-lit kitchen, cleaning up and talking. We were waiting for it to get dark enough for fireworks. Fireflies were starting to tumble and shine in the bushes along the edge of the yard.

"Today isn't July's birthday," Jack said.

"It's not?" Sam stared at me.

"It's okay, man," Jack said, patting Sam's shoulder.

"I never told you that my birthday was on the Fourth of July," I said to Sam.

"Oh," Sam said. "I guess you didn't." He paused. "But I

THE ONLY GIRL IN TOWN

mean, your name? And you invited me over tonight for cake?" He looked confused, his brow furrowed and his eyes searching mine. It was adorable. "Your parents are inside getting it ready?"

"Oh my gosh," I said, putting both of my hands over my mouth. "I did say that, didn't I?" I patted his arm. "I meant this giant cake that looks like an American flag that my mom always makes. You know, with blueberries for the stars and strawberries for the stripes and she puts sparklers in it . . ." I trailed off. "That's what they're inside getting ready. I'm so sorry."

"Um . . ." Sam looked at me, still gripping the box. "So what day *is* your birthday?"

"Well . . ." I let my voice trail off. "My birthday's not even in July."

"Wait." Sam shook his head. "What?"

And then, because I'd answered the next question a million times before and could anticipate it, I went ahead before he could ask. "I was born in May."

"But—"

"I know," I said. "That month is also a name. But my parents didn't use it."

"Why not?"

"I *was* due on the Fourth of July," I told him. "I came way early. May thirty-first. But my parents had been calling me July for months. By the time I was born my parents—my mom especially—were so used to the name, they didn't want to change it."

"Don't feel bad, dude," Jack said. "So many other people have made the same mistake. She's basically running a racket."

"And you really don't have to give me a gift," I said. "You didn't even know me back in May."

"I feel like I've always known you," Sam said, perfectly deadpan. "Go on. Open it."

Carefully, I untied the ribbon and opened the box. Inside was a delicate gold necklace with a small gold circle. A tiny red stone was inset in the middle of the circle, and my initials, *JF*, were stamped on the other side.

"It's beautiful," I said. My voice was soft. I hadn't expected something so nice.

"Ooh, what'd you get?" Jack asked, peering over my shoulder. "Fancy."

"Thank you, Sam," I said, trying to ignore my brother.

"I can't believe you're letting her keep it," Jack said. "When it's not her birthday."

"I'm a really great guy," Sam said. "Also, I don't think I can return it. It's kind of, you know, specific."

"Okay, now I feel bad," I said.

"Don't," Sam said. "It's my fault for assuming it was your birthday. And everyone wants a necklace with a stone that's not actually their birthstone."

"Is it real gold?" Jack wanted to know.

Sam laughed. "Kind of," he said. "It's gold-plated. And the ruby is super small, but it's real."

"Wow," Jack said.

"This is the first real thing anyone other than my family has ever given me." The gift meant a lot to me. I knew how hard Sam was working, trying to supplement his scholarship to Howell.

"It's not like the stone is *that* big," he said, which cracked me up, and he flushed. "I mean, I bought it because I thought it was pretty. Because it seemed like you."

"This is going amazing," Jack said.

"I love it." I handed the necklace to Sam so he could put it on for me. Lifting my hair up, letting him brush the chain and his fingers against my neck, felt more intimate than a kiss.

64.

now

I put Yolo in his cat carrier. He is not pleased.

"Sorry, bud," I say. "Not losing you again."

We drive past the marquee. Nothing has changed.

GET TH3M BACK.

These words. What do they mean?

We drive to Pet Land. The door is unlocked, and it slides open creepily and automatically when we get close. Yolo and I find a cat leash and also one of those cat backpacks that look like they're from space that always made me laugh.

There's not really any way we can pay. There are no cashiers. None of the self-scanners work. No one in the world would blame me for this. While I'm at it, I get some fancy cat food, the kind we bought Yolo for Christmas or when we were feeling extra generous. I also fill the cart with pet toys.

"It's like a shopping spree," I tell Yolo in his cat carrier in the cart. "What have you always wanted?"

Yolo is straight-up pissed now. He's stopped yowling and has turned his back to me. I can just see his butt and tail.

"Fine," I say. "Be like that."

65.

once

"No offense," Syd said, "but you look terrible." She sat down on the edge of the couch. "I thought people were, like, in college when they got their wisdom teeth out."

"I'm special," I said, my speech muffled by cotton. "I'm really mature."

"That you are." Syd began taking things out of the cardboard box she'd brought. "Shake," she said. "Broth." More items. "Pudding. Jell-O."

"Wow," I said.

"Not only did I get you all this stuff," she told me, "but I also drove to buy it."

"Wow," I said again. "You never drive." The medication was making me loopy. I kept repeating things, or the words I was saying weren't quite coming out right.

"I know." She set the Jell-O on the nightstand next to me. It was very jiggly. That was very funny.

"How many days of practice are you going to miss?" Syd asked, when I'd finally stopped laughing.

"None," I said. "I'm good."

"At least three," my mom said from the doorway. She smiled at Syd. "Let me know if you need me. She's definitely still under the influence."

"I am not," I said, but then I giggled again.

"I have a whole plan for today," Syd said. "You're going to eat whatever sounds good, and we're going to watch *Weatheremere*, and I'm going to do a fancy braid in your hair like the one we do for the state meet so you don't have to deal with it at all for the next day or two."

"But I need to be able to sleep on it." I felt very worried. "I'm going to sleep a lot, Syd. A lot." In the doorway, my mom covered her mouth to hide a laugh and that made me mad. "Mom," I said. "It's not funny. I'm going to sleep a lot."

"We know, sweetheart," she said.

"I'll make sure to take sleeping into account when I do the braid," Syd reassured me. "Comfort is our top priority."

"Comfort is our top priority," I informed my mom.

"That's very good to hear," she said, smiling.

I sat up so that Syd could reach my hair. "You must be very good at braiding," I said to her.

"I'm, like, next-level at it," she said, propping up the laptop in front of me. "I did braids soooo many times on my American Girl dolls. And I've braided your hair before."

"You've braided my hair before," I said. I reached for the soup Syd had placed on my nightstand.

The intro for *Weatheremere* started to roll, and the main character flashed across the scene.

"He's hot," I said.

"Yes, very," she said.

"You're like the sister I always wanted," I said, closing my eyes. Her fingers felt so good in my hair.

"The best friend you never knew you needed," she joked back.

"You. Are. The. Actual. Best," I told her with absolute sincerity as Duke Cavanaugh strode onto the screen.

But I could not keep my eyes open, even though the Duke was hotter than humanly possible. Having my hair braided was so soothing. The soup in my stomach was so nice and warm. The pain medication was so effective.

"I love you, Sydney Thompson," I told her.

"I love you, July Fielding," she said, and then I fell asleep.

66.

now

Yolo is OVER IT. He doesn't even *meh* the whole way home. I'm definitely getting the silent treatment.

When we get back from Pet Land something is sitting on my doorstep that wasn't there before.

I think.

I swear.

I forgot to turn on the porch lights and so it's hard to tell what it is exactly.

My heart is racing.

There.

Sitting on my doorstep.

A plastic bucket, the kind we used to pick berries, wiped out and empty.

67.

once

"What do you think?" Syd asked me, sliding into the front seat and opening up a bag.

"Wow," I said, peering inside. "They look great." She'd printed out all the manifestos on a parchment-y looking paper, rolled them up, and secured them with hair ties—blue and gold, the school colors—so we could give them to the other girls on the team.

"Open one," she said, sliding the hair tie off a rolled-up manifesto. "I want you to get the full effect. This one can be yours."

I carefully unfurled the paper. Something about the font looked familiar.

"I took that pledge book from the fraternity to the print shop and asked them to match the font as closely as possible," Syd said. "They got really close, don't you think?"

They had.

"I wanted it to look really cool and old and traditional." Her voice was earnest. "So the girls would feel like they're part of something bigger than themselves. You know?"

"Yeah," I said. "It's great." I was scanning the manifesto. There, in the middle, were a few unfamiliar lines. I glanced up at Syd.

"I added a couple of sentences in the middle," Syd said. "I hope that's okay."

"Yeah, of course," I said, though my voice was tight. So it hadn't been "perfect" after all.

"I've already dropped them off to everyone but the freshmen," Syd said, and I felt a pang of guilt, my annoyance dissipating. I was supposed to have been helping her a couple of hours before. But one thing had led to another with Sam, and I'd shown up so late.

She'd done all this work. And the lines weren't something I would have thought of or dared to write, but they weren't bad.

"I'm sorry," I said. "Seriously."

"It's fine," Syd said. "I swung by Alex's while I was at it."

"How's that going?"

"Well," Syd said. "If I'm honest, it's not going apace."

That made me laugh.

"Maybe you could put in a good word for me?" she asked. She had the window down and was weaving her hand up and down, up and down, through the warm night air.

"What do you want me to say?"

"That you want him to go out with me," she said. "That I'm your best friend."

"You don't need any help from me," I said. "You're Sydney Freaking Thompson. Everyone loves you. But be nice to Alex."

"I always am," she said. "Nice. You know that."

"I do," I said. And she usually was.

Syd reached into her bag and pulled out an apple.

"You've got to be kidding me," I said. "Again? When does this end?"

"Never." Syd grinned, polishing the apple on her white blouse. She peeled off the sticker and stuck it on the glove compartment.

"You're so weird," I told her. "Someday I'm going to actually peel all of those off my car."

"For real, though." Syd turned to look at me. Her face was aglimmer in the lights from the dashboard and the street. She took a bite of the apple and spoke around it. "So who *is* your best friend? Me or Alex?"

"Well, I've known Alex longer," I said, trying to make it sound teasing. Because I didn't know. Who did I love more, Syd or Alex? Who did I need more? What would it mean for me if they were together? Would I lose them both, or would it be fine?

"But I've known you better," Syd said.

In some ways that was true.

Sydney and I slept in the same bed on cross-country and track trips, sometimes laughing until we cried, sometimes falling asleep midsentence. I knew what her legs looked like from the back when she started to sprint. I knew the curve of her cheek and chin when she turned away. On long bus trips, we'd fall asleep on each other's shoulders. I knew what her face looked like when she smiled without knowing she was going to.

"Can you remind me where to turn?" I asked. "I'm not sure where everyone lives." She didn't answer. "Syd? Hello?"

Syd was staring out the window. She was gone, there with me in the car but missing for a moment. Then I saw her come back to herself, reinhabit her body. But some of her electricity was lessened, the thrum and hum of her that had been there moments ago subdued, gone deep, even though she tried to make her voice sound mischievous. "You don't have to do anything yet. Just stay on this road."

68.

now

"We can't have you getting lost," I tell Yolo. I'm wrestling him into a cat harness that attaches to a leash. "What if something attacked you? And this way you don't have to be in the carrier or the backpack." I ignore my own irrationality. Sure, he found his way home. Sure, there no longer seem to be any cars that might hit him or people who might steal him or other animals that might hurt him.

But I have to keep him safe.

Yolo curls up in the back seat to sulk, butt facing me, as is his custom now.

Taylor Farms is on a different road out of town, one I actually haven't tried since everyone disappeared.

I wonder if we're even going to be able to get there. But although it's kind of far out, it's still Lithia. So maybe this *will* work.

As the drive lengthens and the miles pass, Yolo sits up. Soon, he's got his paws on the window, looking out.

"Is this farther than you've ever been, buddy?" I ask him.

He deigns to *meh* at this.

"I know, right?" I say. "Pretty cool."

Where else can I go that I haven't tried yet?

69.

Therapist: *You have to stop tormenting yourself.*

July:

Therapist: *You didn't know what would happen. You didn't know how you'd feel.*

July: *I knew. I knew I was making the wrong decisions. But I didn't know how to stop. And*

I just

didn't

realize

the consequences.

70.

now

"You didn't make this easy," I call out to Syd/Sam/Alex/whoever it might be.

There are so many fields at Taylor Farms. Do I have to walk up and down the rows of each one? Where the strawberries grew in June, where the blueberries and raspberries were in July?

Well. It's not as if I have other ways to spend my time. This is the farthest I've been since everyone disappeared. This far out, the stars are very bright. It's beautiful.

The flashlight I brought from the glove compartment plays on the bushes, making them flash gold and gray, light and dark. It's August now, so the berries are picked over, but every now and then I catch a decaying blueberry, a missing-toothed raspberry, on the vine.

Up and down the rows we walk, Yolo high-key annoyed by and low-level resigned to his leash.

I think I'm in the right place. I don't think I have to go to the farm's orchards for apples.

Because those are fall harvests.

And everything happened in the summer.

71.

once

Freshman year, the last Friday of the summer.

It was now or never.

We were partway through the run. We'd come up the gorge and around the lake and were starting to stride it out by Flat-rock.

"It's okay if you never do it," Alex said. He'd hung back from running with the other guys to run with me. "It's not, like, a thing."

"It's totally a thing," I said.

"Chelsea Hansen hasn't jumped and she's definitely not going to," he pointed out.

"I know, but Chelsea Hansen is a senior and she belongs anyway," I said.

"Exactly my point," Alex said, his arms and legs loose, his voice easy. "She belongs anyway."

"She's not on varsity, though," I told him. "I think to really be on varsity you have to make the jump." I was running well, good enough to make varsity as a freshman, but I knew I would never totally belong if I didn't jump.

"You're getting all superstitious," Alex said. "You don't really believe that, do you? There are other people who haven't jumped. Lots of them."

"A few girls, but none of them are on varsity," I said. "And every freaking guy has done it."

"Huh," Alex said. He was silent for a few strides. "Guys are idiots, though."

"True."

"You don't have to do this unless you want to," Alex said.

A huge heron lifted up over Flatrock.

But here was the thing.

I wanted to do it. I did.

"Today," I said firmly. "If you have any advice, give it to me now."

He was quiet for a while. A quarter of a mile, maybe.

"I think the overthinking is what's getting you," Alex said. "Size it up once today before you go. You know exactly where we all jump from. You've been up there before. Then jump. Don't think. I'll go up there and show you if you want."

"Okay," I said. "Now go ahead and leave me. Get out of here."

He laughed and moved ahead.

I was going to get it the hell over with. I was going to do it fast and then I would be done. No preamble, no drama. Finished. Finally.

I started to pick up my pace.

I caught up with the fastest girls. For the first time ever. I'd been able to run with the second-fastest group, but not the top four, who ran in kind of a loose pack.

"Oh, hey, July," one of them said.

"Hey," I said.

I didn't miss a stride. When we got to the top, they stopped before the cliff's edge to chat with the guys who'd beaten us there. But I kept going.

"Out of my way," I said to the guys. I strode to the cliff edge and looked down. Two guys were in the water already, seniors. "Watch out!" I yelled down to them, and then I walked backward a few steps, paused for a split second, and charged for the cliff's edge.

I didn't even take off my running shoes.

When I surfaced, I looked up. People above were cheering for me. I couldn't tell which one was Alex, exactly, but I knew he was there.

72.

now

And then I see it. The next clue. Like a flag, fluttering ever so slightly in the early morning breeze, catching the light with a white flash.

A Verity napkin, speared on one of the spiky tops of a raspberry bush.

"Verity." I say the word out loud. It means truth.

73.

once

"Hi, Mrs. Harper," Syd said brightly. "Is Morgan here?"

"I'm sorry," Morgan's mom said. "She's not. But she'll be back at—"

"That's actually perfect." Syd interrupted her so smoothly that it didn't even seem like an interruption. She smiled and held out her hand. "I'm Sydney Thompson, and this is July Fielding. We're the girls' cross-country team captains."

"Of course." Morgan's mom beamed, shaking hands with both of us. I'd seen people react like this to Syd before. Her charisma was undeniable.

"We wanted to leave this in her room as a surprise," Syd said, lifting the rolled-up manifesto she held in her other hand. "Would that be okay?"

Wait. What? I hadn't known that was part of the plan. I thought we'd give them to their parents, or leave them on the doorstep, if the girls weren't home. I glanced over at Syd. But Morgan's mom was opening the door wider, stepping back. "Of course," she said. "What a nice thing for you girls to do." She led us to the stairs, which were covered in worn gray carpet. Photos lined the stairway all the way up in mismatched frames. "It's the first door on your right at the top of the stairs."

"Thank you."

"It's probably a mess in there."

Syd started up the steps. "I guarantee you it cannot be worse than my room," she said over her shoulder, and Morgan's mom laughed.

Morgan's door was closed. Syd opened it. It was a small room, with a bed, dresser, and closet. No desk or vanity. Contrary to what Morgan's mom had said, it was fairly tidy. Her bed was made, and no clothes were on the floor or spilling out of the dresser or closet. Her comforter was navy blue, she'd taped photos of different skiers and snowboarders above her desk, and there were a couple of plants on the dresser soaking in the summer light.

"This is, like, the opposite of Ella's room," Syd said, looking around.

"When have you been in Ella's room?" I asked. Being in Morgan's room felt strangely intimate. We weren't really in the stage of life anymore when you went into everyone else's rooms all the time.

"We were hanging out," Syd said airily. "You've been very busy with Sam."

Morgan had used washi tape to put up pictures on the wall next to her bed. Photos of her with a dog; with an older boy, her brother, who'd been in a lot of the photos lining the stairs. A photo of her kayaking, a few of her rock climbing. One of her flashing a victory sign as she sat on top of a dirt bike in full gear.

"Geez," Syd said. "No wonder she was the first to jump this year." She tapped one of the photos of Morgan with her brother.

"Remember him? Tony? I think he graduated the year we were sophomores."

"Yeah." He'd been nice, if I remembered right. He hadn't been a runner, so I didn't know him well.

Syd tucked the rolled-up manifesto under Morgan's pillow. "There." She stepped back. Then she shook her head. "No. I don't want her to squash it." She pulled the manifesto back out and placed it carefully on top of the pillow.

"So, which freshman should we deliver to next?" I asked when we were back in the car. "And when?"

"I don't know," Syd said. "It's really up to them."

And then I understood.

All the upcoming sophomore, junior, and senior girls had already jumped at least once. Some had only gone once, ever. But they'd all done it.

Out of the rising freshmen, Morgan was the only one who'd jumped so far.

I looked at Syd.

The manifesto was supposed to include everyone. Gather them all in. Bring us together as a team.

But Syd was making it all about the jump.

74.

now

The Verity smell hits me the minute I walk inside. That delicious, cold, ice cream scent.

I always swore it soaked into Sam's clothes. That his shirt smelled like vanilla, and that I could taste blackberries on his lips and smell butter pecan in his hair.

Everything is pin-neat, shipshape. The ice cream tubs are full and pristine, waiting for someone to dig into them, and the scoops are lined up neatly, one next to each tub. The glass case shimmers. The red-and-white paper napkins are neatly stacked, as if someone has used a ruler's edge to get them *exactly so*. The red vinyl–padded chairs are tucked in under the round chrome tables. Four chairs to each table.

Yolo is going crazy over by the ice cream, so I scoop him a dish of vanilla, set it on the floor, tie his leash to a chair, and leave him to gorge himself. The back rooms are shiny equipment and tile floors. I hold my breath when I go into the restrooms and check for anything. No messages scrawled on the inside of the stalls. Nothing out of place that I can see.

If I really can get in anywhere, I think, *I should make the most of this. I should go to stores and take whatever I want. I should go to rich people's houses and drink their booze.*

I've never had a drink in my life. Before, I didn't want to mess up my running. After, I didn't want to mess up me.

Any more than I already was, anyway.

Out in the main area again, Yolo is licking his bowl clean. I take a couple of steps back and let my eyes run over the list of flavors. In a movie, this might be where I see the clue. Maybe certain letters would be underlined or shaded, and if I put them all together, it would explain something. Or I'd stare at the flavors and somehow they'd rearrange themselves in front of my eyes.

"I guess we can go," I start to say to Yolo, and that's when it happens.

Again.

That out-of-the-corner-of-my-eye flash. This time near the side door, the one I can't fully see. The bells jingle. The air in the room shifts slightly as a door opens, closes.

Someone just left.

75.

now

"How are they doing this?" I ask Yolo. I'm furious and sweaty and panting because I have been running around a parking lot and up and down the alleys and side streets near Verity carrying a heavy, furry, pissed-off cat in my arms. "I've never heard a car. So they've got to be on foot, right?"

Whoever it is has escaped us again. They always stay just out of view, flickering like a candle, like stars behind clouds.

76.

now

"So where to next?" I ask Yolo, setting him down by my car.

He's straining on his leash back toward Verity's front door. He wants more ice cream.

"We're not going back in," I tell him. They're gone, whoever it was. I might have caught them if I hadn't had to untie Yolo's leash before I could start chasing.

I'd be faster without him.

But I can't risk losing him again.

"We're going to have to give the backpack a shot," I say. "I can run with that thing on."

Yolo looks at me balefully. He's going to hate it. He knows it and I know it. But I have to find whoever it is.

I almost had them here. At Verity.

Verity.

Sam.

What if it's Sam who came back?

If it were, what if he pulled me close? What if he put his mouth on mine and his hands on my hips, that perfect spot he knew, the very edges of his fingers brushing ever so slightly beneath the waistband of my jeans, nothing anyone watching would even notice, but something I felt in every cell of my body?

What if he held me? Let me lean into him? Didn't let go?
It's been so long since I've been held.
Suddenly I'm very sure it's Sam I wished for.

77.

once

LITHIA HERALD ONLINE
HAWKS ON THE RUN

Will the Lithia High Hawks be able to take home an elusive state championship this year?

Since the arrival of Sydney Thompson, the team has been on the rise. During her first year with the team, they moved up from a fifth-place finish the year before to third. Last year, they took second. Could the first state title in Lithia High's history be within their reach?

Thompson, the fastest runner on the team, was also second overall in the state last year.

"Our team was able to place so high because we have such a solid base of runners behind Sydney," Coach Warren said. "July Fielding finished ninth overall and second on our team, and our next few girls came in right after her."

And keep an eye on Ella Kane. The freshman phenom has been running well all summer. "She's already running faster times than Sydney did as a sophomore," Coach Warren said. "We've known she was coming up thanks to her middle school coach, but frankly, she's surprised us all. She's pure talent. She truly loves to run."

Warren also added, "I think it really speaks to the camaraderie of this team and the leadership of the older girls that she's running at such a high level so soon. Without a challenge, talent can stall out. We've just begun to see what Ella can do."

And, when asked how she felt about the team's chances, and her chances of winning State this year, Thompson said, "The only number I'm aiming for is one."

78.

now

I stop at home and wrestle Yolo into the cat backpack. For the first time in his life, he scratches me, neat red marks along my arms. "Hey," I say, harsher than I mean to. He stops, looks up at me with wide eyes.

"Sorry," I say.

He's quiet.

No *meh*.

We both feel bad.

I think.

"I know," I say. "This isn't ideal. Just see this through with me. Okay?"

I can't stop now.

79.

once

"Shhh," I told Sam when I opened the Millers' door.

I'd never had a boy over while I was babysitting before. But the kids were all asleep. I had tucked them in, I'd read them stories, we'd eaten Push Pops on the patio and made a town in the tangled part of the yard by setting out rocks in squares for houses and lines for roads.

And then Sam texted me—*Any chance I can see you tonight?*—and the kids were all asleep and I wanted to see him so much. As he came up the walk, something about the way he looked at me, as I held the door open for him, told me that it was one of those moments, deep blue as a starred night sky. If you don't stop and stand and stay in it, looking up, you will miss it completely.

"I really, really needed to see you," he said, laughing, his face buried in my neck. He'd changed his clothes from Verity, but I could swear I still smelled ice cream in his hair. "I couldn't wait until tomorrow. I know I'm being ridiculous."

I smiled, even though he was now kissing my mouth.

Sam and I were hungry for each other. We pressed up against the wall near the door, where we'd be out of view if any of the kids wandered in.

Sam stopped and glanced up at the bookshelves in the corner of the room.

I followed his gaze.

"They don't have a nanny cam or anything, do they?" he asked.

"I don't think so," I said. They'd never told me they had one, anyway. Although once Sam brought it up, I realized he had a point. I wouldn't put it past Hannah Miller. She was conscientious in every possible way.

I had an idea. I took his hand and led him out into the backyard, where globe lights strung on trees bobbed in the wind. Rain was on the way.

"Yeah," Sam said, "this works," and he pulled me down on the outdoor couch. I tucked in against him, even though it wasn't cold and the rain wasn't coming down yet. It was the swirl before the storm, when leaves are on the move and clouds cover and uncover the moon and stars. I loved the feel of Sam's chest against my back, of my knees tucked right up against his.

I felt perfectly relaxed in his arms. We fit together. I wanted to ask him out loud the thing I'd been wondering all summer.

"How come you like me?" I asked Sam. "You could be with college girls. You could have Syd."

"You're more dangerous," he said.

I laughed.

"I'm serious," Sam said. He shifted again, and I turned to face him, resting my head on his chest. His hand found my hair. I closed my eyes at his touch, at his voice, low and warm and near my ear. "Don't you know how dangerous you are?"

80.

now

"Sorry, bud," I tell Yolo. "We might be here a few minutes."

I set down Yolo's backpack against one of the beds in Sam's dorm room, and then I straight-up go through Sam's things without any guilt. I'm interested to see what he's kept. Who he has become in the time since we've seen each other.

I'm shameless, hungry for any details of his life. Who did he date? How did he do in his classes? Who were his friends? Are there any pictures? Was Howell everything he thought it would be?

I recognize some of the T-shirts. Not all. One Verity T-shirt, which he probably wears ironically now.

I find a Howell hoodie, worn and soft. When I lift it up, it smells like Sam, the soap he used. Underneath that, another sweatshirt, with an emblem—logo—on it that looks familiar.

In the split second it takes me to cross the room and pick up the hoodie, I've got it.

It's the Alpha Kappa Sigma letters. One of them, the sigma, resembles an angular *E*. A backward *3*.

So, Sam must have joined that frat. You think you know a guy. How funny. Is that funny? I'm not sure. I know everyone went on without me over the past year. Kept running, kept

THE ONLY GIRL IN TOWN

trying new things, kept going. The team took State without me. They didn't need me after all.

I pull the Howell sweatshirt on over my head and tuck my hands up inside the sleeves, which are too long.

This is stealing, but is it? It's a survival thing. It's like if you're on a polar expedition and everyone else dies, it's okay to take their food and clothes and supplies and whatever. Definitely don't eat their bodies, I mean, but you can for sure take their stuff.

I walk to the window and look out at all the glittering lights of my empty town. I can *see* the places I can't go, including the other side of Route 13. I can just about pinpoint where my car stopped when I tried to drive out of town that first night after everyone disappeared.

I hear Yolo moving around in his backpack. Something in the air in the room seems to shift.

I peel my eyes away from the window. Yolo starts yowling. "What is it, buddy?"

He's going crazy in the backpack, squirming in the direction of the door.

Down the hall, the elevator dings.

81.

once

"May," my mom would say, laughing. "You could never be named May."

It's pretty enough, she would say. But you are July. You are fireworks and summer thunderstorms. A scatter of stars in the sky. The smoke from a bonfire.

May is the word you use when you're asking permission, she said. You have never waited to ask permission.

82.

now

I dart down the hallway, backpack bouncing, Yolo yowling. I take the turn to the elevator lobby too fast and almost fall, but catch myself before I do. I skid to a stop in front of the elevator.

The display shows that it's going down.

Of course. Nowhere to go but.

I dart a glance in the direction of the stairwell. Would that be faster?

I don't know what to do. Yolo writhes on my back, I was *this close* to seeing them—

I sprint for the stairs.

I'm gonna get you.

83.

once

Before everything, there was a day when the three of us ran together. When I kept up without even having to try.

It was raining, that misty, heavy, relentless summer rain that I loved in spite of myself, that felt like it was turning the world green again. You could feel it in your skin. We were beyond drenched, so wet that water ran off our elbows in streams. Our shoes were heavy, our legs slick.

Running that day, we were perfectly in sync.

Syd.

Ella.

Me.

We didn't speak.

There was nothing to say.

84.

now

I take the stairs two at a time.

I reach the stairwell of the first floor. Up to the next, or down to the basement? Where have they gone? I pause and listen, even though my pounding heart screams at me to *go, go, go!*

Thump. Thump. Thumpthumpthump.

The sound is coming from below.

I race down the stairs.

Th-thump, th-thump, th-thump thump.

Louder and louder the closer I come.

What is it?

Who is it?

I take a deep breath, sling Yolo in his backpack higher on my back.

THUMP. THUMP. THUMP.

A hallway, at the bottom of the stairs.

A door, slightly ajar.

The room is dim, lit by rows of flickering fluorescent lights. The corners are dark, and I play my phone light over them. Cobwebs, what looks like a dead mouse, a stiff straw broom, a bottle of an electric green cleaning liquid. That's all.

Except for several washing machines and dryers in the middle of the back wall.

That's where the sound is coming from. One of the dryers.

Something's inside.

I cross the room, taking a look back over my shoulder. I don't want to get trapped in here.

I'm also not sure I want to know what's inside the dryer.

"Keep your eyes on the door, Yolo," I say. "Don't let anyone shut it on us." And then I jerk open the door of the dryer and the sound comes to a stop. Breathing fast, I look inside, my stomach churning.

A pair of running shoes.

They're mine.

85.

once

Once, Sam and I went to the jump when it was dark.

People liked to go at night, even though it was more dangerous then. We all knew the warnings.

Don't jump from the cliff ever. But especially not at night.

You can't see how deep it is.

You could break your back.

You could break your neck.

But Sam and I didn't go at night. We went so early that no one else was there.

If you want to sneak out, if you want to be with someone, you can go at three or four in the morning. Those are secret hours. They seem to exist out of time entirely, or else very deep inside it.

Sam had a flashlight that he kept low. He held my hand the whole way. When we walked through the grassy field that smelled like rain, even though there hadn't been a storm for days. When we brushed through the bushes that sounded of crickets. When we went into the trees, carefully felt our way to the cliff, looked down.

When we jumped.

He left the flashlight on the cliff, so we only had light from

the moon and stars, but we found each other without any trou-
ble at all.

My hand on his wet skin. His breath in the hollow by my
shoulder. And I knew I'd been wrong before, about feeling everything I could possibly feel.

Because, this.

Him.

Me.

When we came here together.

The stars high. The air heavy.

The dark water slipping over.

Him.

Me.

Again.

Again.

This was

everything

anyone

could ever feel.

86.

now

"We don't have to keep playing their game," I tell Yolo, as we pull into the parking lot of the high school. "Looking for clues. Running all over town. We're going to cut to the chase."

We climb out of the car. Yolo's claws click-clack on the tile of the school hallway. He's pleased to be on his leash instead of in the backpack. He deserves a break. Yolo keeps his eyes straight ahead as we walk into the main office.

He knows we're on a mission.

GET TH3M BACK.

I try the security footage first, but there's nothing. The file is deleted, the computer wiped bare. I expected this. Whoever it is has caught on to us.

It could be Sam. Or Syd. Alex. Or Ella. Jack.

The first clue, the apple sticker, pointed to Syd. She was the one who ate them. But everyone else knew about them. Ella, Alex, and Sam had all been in the car when she stuck them on the glove compartment. Jack, too, come to think of it.

The baseball. On the surface, that seemed like Jack. He was the one who played. But Syd and Ella and I had hidden in the dugout, and Alex had been looking for us. And we'd told the story to Sam, how Ella had saved us from getting caught that night.

The berry bucket. That's another tough one. Everyone who's ever lived in Lithia has gone berry picking there. The Miller kids were more the exception than the rule, because they were new. And I know I'd told Sam about the farms.

Next, the Verity napkin. Sam worked there, but it was just as likely to be Alex. We went to Verity long before Sam even moved here. We were the ones eating our way through the menu.

The running shoes, at Sam's dorm, had been next. And we had all been together, running, or right after, at some point. Except Jack. But would I really have wished for a family member, anyway?

Yes. I would have. Everyone is missing.

So.

What if.

What if it really is more than one person.

What if they're *all* here?

87.

once

It was raining the spring of our junior year, and Syd and I were standing outside of Wegmans with our takeout cartons, waiting for it to clear up before we ran to the car. A bunch of other people were doing the same thing with their groceries.

Some fiftysomething guy came up to us with an umbrella, and he told us to take it

even though it was clear it was his only one and that now he

would be the one getting soaked

even if he were just walking to his car

and Syd and I were like thank you thank you

and an elderly woman behind us who already had an umbrella said how nice he was, how kind that was and

someone behind her agreed

and everyone standing under the store's overhang was alight with the kindness of his gesture

and he smiled and said, "got to keep the pretty ones dry" and as he was standing there basking in the glow of his good deed he looked back at me and Syd and winked and said so the rest of the line couldn't hear

"actually, it wouldn't be *too* bad if you girls got wet"

he said that

they do that. They say things and look, sometimes when they mean to and sometimes when they don't, men who think of themselves as *red-blooded* and *all-American* and *good-guy.* They go so fast from *I would never* to *So what if I did?* They do it and then they tell themselves that they didn't, or that if they did, it's fine. They're fine. They've never been anything but fine.

anyway

he said that

and

Syd's eyes met mine

and we knew we were feeling the same way

and she

dropped the umbrella on the ground

and we walked off in the rain without looking back, and then

we were running,

and then

we were laughing

and I don't know

that

I have ever loved anyone more.

88.

now

I've been trying. I've been chasing them all over town, whoever it is, however many of them there are. Trying to catch them.

But. I think I know how to do it. I have a new idea.

The student government room is another place I avoided last year, so as Yolo and I walk across the room, I notice banners and signs I haven't seen before, handwriting I don't recognize on the whiteboard.

At the end of my junior year, I ran for class secretary again, and I won. But after everything that happened, I just sort of never showed up. I never went to anything or did anything or responded to any texts about it. They'd put someone else in my place.

The markers are lined up neatly in the tray of the whiteboard. The minifridge, when I open it, is still full of off-brand diet soda, and the cupboard next to it has Nature Valley crunchy granola bars, the nourishment the school provided us. Nobody ever ate them unless we were desperate.

We'd spent so many hours in here junior year, Alex and me.

"I bet other schools have, like, fancy printers and graphic design stuff they can use instead," I'd say, as we wore out another marker coloring in lettering for a poster announcing a band concert or a debate trip.

"I bet other schools have a lot of things," Alex muttered.

But at Lithia High we always liked that we were scrappy.

I open the cupboard where we used to keep the marquee letters.

In addition to not having enough *Es*, we also didn't have a question mark, so we used the money sign instead. The best was one time when a guy on the football team used the marquee to ask a girl to a dance. In order to fit all the words on the marquee he spaced them out like this:

SOPHIA WILL YOU GO TO

HOM3COMING WITH M3 $KEVIN

So from then on Syd started calling him MoneyKevin, and it stuck.

But Kevin had a ton of confidence. He could handle the nickname. He embraced it, in fact.

I haven't thought about MoneyKevin in ages. I wonder where he is now.

I wonder where they *all* are now. The ones I haven't thought about since this happened.

The ones who didn't matter as much to me as

the ones I can't live without.

89.

once

"You're a mess." Jack hung over the chain-link fence, grinning, sweaty, one game behind him, one game to come. The grass of the baseball field was almost luminescent green, thanks to the way the dusky light was hitting it slantwise. It was a hot, humid, late-summer evening.

"Thanks a lot," I said. I'd gotten done with a solo evening run. Sweat was dripping down my back, and my hair had started to frizz out from its ponytail. "Be nice to me or you won't get this." I held out the Gatorade I'd gotten him, lime cucumber, his favorite. I'd put it in in the freezer a couple of hours before so it was part slush, the way he liked it.

Jack and I went to each other's stuff as often as we could. Spring was tricky, because the high school track and baseball seasons were at the same time, but I went to lots of his summer league games, and in the fall he came to lots of my cross-country meets.

"I take everything back," Jack said. "You look great. Amazing."

"Did you guys win your first game?"

"Yeah," he said. "Gonna win this one, too." His coach called something out to him, and I tossed the Gatorade over the fence, my aim perfect because I was used to lobbing balls at Jack for him to hit. He caught it in one hand.

"Show-off," I said. After Jack was gone, I looked into the stands for my dad. He wasn't hard to find, standing up to stretch, wearing the ball cap he'd had for as long as I could remember.

I climbed up into the bleachers next to him. "How's Jack been playing?"

"Great," Dad said. "He had a double last at-bat, and his fielding's been good."

"Where's Mom?"

"Book club," Dad said. "She left after the first game." He looked down at me with his kind, crinkly-edged eyes. "I'm going to get a hot dog. Want one?"

"Sure."

"I'll be right back. You save our seats."

I sat down among the other parents and siblings, waving to a few I knew. It was cooling off, turning into a gorgeous night. The teams took the field. Jack was hitting first, and within a few minutes, it was his turn.

I glanced over in the direction of the snack shack to see how close my dad was. Did he know Jack was at bat?

He did.

Of course he did. He always timed his refreshment runs so he could walk along the fence without getting told to move along. That way he could be closer to Jack, see the swing better. They'd talk about it later, go over it in the backyard, whatever the outcome. Bad or good. My dad was walking slowly, a hot dog in each hand, his eyes on my brother.

Jack tapped his bat on the ground, taking his time. He looked so relaxed, easy. I knew that feeling in a different way. When I was striding it out right at the beginning of a race and could tell it was going to be a good one.

My phone buzzed. I tucked it away. I was going to be here now.

CRACK.

SHOOM.

Jack's bat connected with the ball at the exact moment that the lights came on.

I flew up, arms in the air. "YES!"

My dad and I looked at each other across the bleachers, grinning.

Jack loped to third, easy as pie, that frustrating, beautiful stride that would make him such a good runner if only he'd ever give it a shot.

My heart cracked, too. It was so good to be there.

I never wanted

to be gone.

90.

now

The plastic letters that go up on the marquee are bigger than you'd think. They're larger than your hand, like eight inches tall. Ours are covered in fine scratches that are hard to see unless you're up close. The box they came in disappeared long ago, so we keep them in a plastic storage bin, where they slide and scatter around. Every now and then someone tries to organize them. But it would all become a mess again.

It drove Alex nuts.

There's the bin I want. *Marquee* is written on the outside in thick black Sharpie that is starting to fade.

I open the bin.

Crap.

The letters are all gone.

Of course they are.

I start to laugh. "It's okay," I say. "I've got it now."

Wherever you might be hiding.

Whoever you might be.

However many of you there might be.

I've got *you* now.

91

Today was my birthday. For it I got:
- A bike (from Mom and Dad)
- A box of my favorite cereal (from Dad) (he does this every year) (my favorite is Apple Jacks but you're allowed to change it if you want to) (next year I might pick Cocoa Puffs)
- A book (from Mom)
- A scooter (from Grammy and Papa)
- A bag of Skittles (from Jack)

And this is the best part of all. I saved it until the end. I also got:
- a cat.

—Journal entry by July Fielding, age nine.

92.

now

"This is like student government," I tell Yolo. "Getting high off Sharpie fumes making a poster."

But I'm not making a poster. I'm making my own letters since the plastic ones are gone. I've cut white paper into pieces that are approximately the right size, and I'm trying to make the letters look as close to the originals as possible. It's a huge hassle to color it all in, and I'm running out of time.

I'm making just enough letters to say what I want to say.

93.

once

In English we read a poem.

It was called "Naming of Parts."

The man who wrote it was a soldier in World War II and he was naming the parts of his gun as he got ready but the natural world never went away

he was naming the parts of his gun but the natural world was not affected

sure

the soldiers dug trenches and ruined earth and blew holes in trees

but it turns out the world kept on going and grew over it

I think that's what the poem meant anyway

the teacher said something like that.

I could never pay full attention to anything after last summer so I can't be totally sure.

But that seems right.

If we died the world could still grow over us

still

after all we've done.

94.

now

GET TH3M BACK.

I've been saying their names in my mind.

I could list them up on the marquee.

Like I did on that pink Post-it my therapist gave me.

Mom

Dad

Jack

Sydney

Sam

Alex

Ella

Yolo

I've been trying. I've been remembering all the things I've done wrong. I've been going over and over the summer I spent the last year trying to forget.

Yolo is already here.

And who else?

It could be all of them.

It could be one of them.

The one I want the most.

Which one would that be?

I'd say the same thing to any of them that I've been saying over and over and over again for the past year. But maybe this time, it will work. Maybe this time, it will be enough.

I have enough letters to spell

I'm sorry.

95.

once

It was May 31 and I was fourteen, reading a book in the bathtub, with a big slice of cake and a huge scoop of ice cream on the edge of the tub next to me. It was a book my mom had given me for my birthday the year I started hearing the cold lonely sound. She had read it, too, when she was younger. It was her very own favorite copy.

It had a sunset-colored cover with a watercolor of a small house on a lake. Her name was written on the inside cover, and the edges were wavy with water damage from when I'd dropped it in the bathtub once before. There were eleven marks on the inside, one for each time I'd read it. I read it a bunch when I first got it and then every year on my birthday. The book was called *Tuck Everlasting*, and it was about a girl who met a family who could never die.

"July, come on," Jack said. "I have to get in. I left my cleats in there."

I glanced over. His baseball cleats were, indeed, under the sink.

"It's my birthday," I said. "I get to do whatever I want. And I don't want to get out yet."

"I have practice," he moaned. "Pleeaaase."

"I'll be out in five minutes if you leave me alone," I said.

I could tell by the silence on the other side of the door that we might have a deal.

After I put a spoonful of chocolate ice cream into my mouth, I turned the page.

I read *Tuck Everlasting* every year because I loved it, and because I hoped that if I read it enough, the idea of dying not being the worst possible thing would rub off on me. And I read it every year on my birthday, May 31, because that felt right.

I turned the page again. There it was, one of my favorite parts, when Tuck explains to Winnie, the heroine, why he wishes he could go back and become mortal again.

You can't have living without dying. So you can't call it living, what we got. We just are, we just be, like rocks beside the road.

I thought of things like this as handholds. Reading a book on my birthday, running in the morning, making Rice Krispie treats with my dad on Sunday afternoons and eating them straight out of the pan, playing video games with Jack, going rock climbing with my mom. That was probably what had given me the idea to call them handholds, actually.

They were the things I could hold on to so I could keep from falling.

96.

now

I stand at the bottom of the marquee and look up.

IM SORRY

In the light from the floodlight, I can just make out the words. It looks like one of those cut-out letter messages that kidnappers send. Even though I tried to make my letters uniform, they're all off a bit, a slightly crazy tilt to the leg of my *M*, a lopsided *O*. And they're not quite dark enough to be seen well. And the paper is too thin. And I forgot to make an apostrophe.

I've tied Yolo to the bottom of the marquee. "Not great, right?" I say to him, and he glares up at me.

As I stand there, the Y from IM SORRY flutters to the ground.

"Oh, *come on*," I say.

97.

"Mindfulness teachers say that impermanence terrifies us, but that we don't need to be afraid of it or think of it as a bad thing," my therapist said. "Do you know why that might be?"

I didn't answer. The Post-its on her desk were bright yellow that day. Where had all the pink ones gone? Were there now pink squares all over town with people's most important people written on them?

"It's because without impermanence, there is no growth," the therapist said.

I saw a pink Post-it then. It was at the edge of her desk. It had Don't forget to mail taxes written on it.

It did not mean anything.

98.

now

I pick up the *Y* and climb the ladder to put it back.

I stick it up again, pressing the tape hard this time, and then I lean back ever so slightly to look at my handiwork. Something catches my eye, and I realize that Yolo has untied himself. He's sneaking away. "YOLO!" I scream. I forget that no one is holding the ladder, I forget that I'm even *on* a ladder, and down I go.

My back hits a tree root so hard the pain literally blinds me. I can't breathe. Am I broken?

A few seconds pass. Air comes back into my lungs. I can see again.

I lift up my arm, the one that hurts the most. There's a wide, long patch where the skin has come clear off and it's down to the meat of me, slick and red and so stripped it's not even bleeding yet.

"Did you see that?" I yell at whoever is out there. "Do you care? Is there anything that could happen to me that would make you come *help* me?"

Something nudges at me.

Yolo.

He may have untied himself, but he didn't run off.

"Thank you," I tell him. I reach out my uninjured arm and grab his leash.

He climbs up to sit on my chest, staring. I know I have to get up and get going, but for a moment it hurts too much. Maybe we could just stay here for tonight, on this cool grass, suspended. I lie there, looking past Yolo at what I've written.

IM SORRY

I can tell one thing now—whatever this is that's happening with this town and these letters and this mess and with me

I can hurt *more*

I can die.

99.

once

When I was twelve or thirteen, I made my mom mad. I can't remember what I said, only that it was terrible and personal, and I knew it. I knew I had gone beyond the pale, pushed the limits too hard. I ran to my room and shut the door behind me and, because I knew she could pick the lock with an unbent hanger to get it open, I braced myself with my back against the mirror hung on the back of my door. I put my feet against the desk.

She picked the lock. And then she couldn't push it open.

Look at that, I thought. *Look at that, I'm stronger than her.*

Then she started kicking the door. She kicked it over and over, sharp kicks, yelling something at me. My back thudded with the impact, but I braced my legs harder. I did not give way.

Another kick, harder than the others. Another, harder than that.

The mirror shattered all around me.

I screamed.

My mom stopped.

"Oh no," she said. "July? July? What happened?"

"The mirror broke," I said.

"Oh no," my mom said again. "Are you cut?"

"No," I said. I wasn't, but I didn't know what would happen if I moved.

"Stay right there," she said. "Hold still."

A few moments later my mother appeared at my window, her face tear-streaked, a garbage bag in her hand. She pushed the screen in and climbed inside.

"July," she said. "I'm so sorry."

She cried the whole time, picking up the pieces and dropping them into the garbage bag with her bare hands. "Hold on," she said. "Don't move. I don't want you to get cut."

I held so still.

"I'm sorry," she said. "I'm so sorry."

I could tell she was.

"I've never done anything like that before," she said.

She was right. She hadn't.

"I won't again," she said.

I believed her.

There was glass in my hair.

I glittered.

100.

now

Please.
Can't this be enough?
These words?
I mean them with all my heart.

101.

once

In another poem
    this one by Ross Gay
    his niece, who is young, cries
    because she had a butterfly friend she named Emma
    who flew away
    and the niece never got to say goodbye.
    Would it
    even help, though,
    if they came back so you could?
    (say goodbye)
    Or would you just hold on hold on hold on
    and never ever let go
    until
    they took you with them.

102.

now

"I know this is gross," I tell Yolo. Blood drips from my arm onto the seat of the car. Something happened to my leg in the fall that I hope is temporary. My head still hurts in the back, a low, dull ache from where it hit the ground. But the message is up. We've done what we can.

"For now," I tell Yolo, "all we have to do is get back home."

Yolo blinks at me from the backpack.

"Hey," I tell Yolo. "Thanks for sticking with me. Thanks for not running off when you had the chance."

103.

now

Yolo and I finally pull into my driveway. There should be people sleeping, living in every house I pass.

Instead, for now, there is just me. And water, stone, trees. The town. Me, the only girl in it. The only person here.

No. Not true.

Someone else is here. I'm doing it. I'm getting them back. Like the sign said.

Aren't I?

104.

now

"This is going to sting," I tell Yolo. Our eyes meet in my parents' bathroom mirror. "You might want to avert your eyes if you don't want to see me suffer."

He stares at me the entire time I clean the wound and slather on the Neosporin and careful, careful put on a bandage.

"We don't want to run the risk of infection," I say to Yolo. "That could be fatal."

And then I laugh.

Because, really, what could be worse than this?

Even dying

might

be better

than being so

alone.

105.

now

I climb back under the vanity in my parents' bathroom.

I've gathered a few things in with me over the past couple of days. The blankets and pillows, which make sleeping okay, if not exactly comfortable. I brought the clues. The apple sticker. The baseball, the berry bucket, the napkin. My old running shoes. Everything that led me all over town and back again. I'm still wearing Sam's hoodie because it feels like I can't quite get warm.

I don't like going into my room. It's too big, too full of who I used to be and then wasn't anymore.

Yolo wads himself up next to me. I'm so freaking glad he's here. I put my hand on his head and he leans into it. "Okay," I say. "We need to get some rest. And then, we'll go see what they said."

Yolo's got nothing.

"That's okay," I say. "Me either, buddy."

106.

once

Ella had texted, asking me to come over. We were sitting on her bed. Her room still seemed like a tween's room—pink and purple and posters of cute boys in small bands.

It was the second-to-last Fall Creek Friday of the summer. Everyone else had jumped. Everyone else was wearing the hair ties. Everyone else was in.

Ella was the fastest girl on the team, next to Syd. But she was out. Because she hadn't jumped.

Was that why Syd had done it? I wondered. When she saw Ella getting faster and faster, did she decide to make the jump more of a thing? So that Ella still wouldn't belong in some important way?

It was strange that, with all the time we'd spent together, that was the first time I'd been in Ella's room. Syd had already been there. Which was strange, too.

Looking more closely, I noticed some pictures from the summer printed out and tacked to the wall. I saw a throw pillow that looked new. It was a navy-blue shibori pattern instead of fluffy and soft.

It was the room of someone who was in the process of turning into someone else. Someone who would gain things, sure, but who would also leave parts of herself behind.

I'd already given Ella all the advice Alex had given me before I jumped for the first time. She was one of the first up to the top every Friday, because she was one of the fastest. But then, week by week, everyone else jumped and she didn't. I was waiting for her in the water, but she never came down.

"You don't have to do it, ever," I said, there in her room. "Like, ever."

"Yes, I do."

I understood. I'd been there before.

Ella's jaw was set. "There's nothing worse than failing in front of everyone."

There was something worse, actually.

It was not committing to the jump. If you ran for the edge and then stopped, or hesitated, or jumped halfheartedly, you wouldn't get far enough.

If you didn't go hard, if you mistimed the leap at all, you could break on the rocks below.

107.

now

Yolo snuggles up close, and I start to sing him songs.

Yolo only ever likes it when I sing, not my mom or dad or Jack, because my voice is not too high, not too low; it's just right. It's the Baby Bear of voices for Yolo.

I sing him the song my mom used to sing me, but with his name. *Yolo, Yolo Fielding. Yolo, Yolo Fielding.* I sing him "Rock-a-bye Baby" and a song about cat food that I make up and then an old song by Bruce Springsteen called "Downbound Train" that my dad loved.

I had a job, I had a girl

I had something going, mister, in this world

That last song is pretty sad, but I've always liked it and Yolo does, too.

He's purring, curled into a warm comma in my lap. "Are you lonely?" I ask him. "Do you wish there were other cats to hang out with?"

He purrs harder, kneads his claws into my thigh.

He doesn't. He only needs me.

I'm enough.

My heart fills.

It's not an enormous world, this one town, but also it is. It is every house every tree every pocket of space underneath a bush.

Every chair sitting on the sidewalk outside a restaurant, every swing in every park.

No one else is here and so all of it is ours.

"You've got a point," I tell Yolo. "It's not all bad."

As I think about my town, the lights that come on later as the sun will set tomorrow night, the last night, as I think about the starlight that will shine through when it's dark (*click*, says God, and on the stars go), I feel the most dangerous thing.

What if I get used to this?

What if I give up?

It would be

it will be

so much easier

if

I just don't care anymore.

I don't care anymore.

No.

I'm too close.

I have to see this through.

108

Therapist: *You're not a bad person. You've made some choices that you wish you could go back and change. That's something that every human being on this planet does during their lifetime.*

July: *Not like this.*

Therapist:

July:

Therapist: *And those choices have compounded and compounded. One small thing can snowball. It can feel impossible to get out from under it. But you can.*

July:

Therapist: *Your choices do not define you. You can move forward with greater knowledge. You can heal.*

July:

Therapist: *The focus should always be on the kind of person you want to become, not on any particular outcome. You can't change anything but yourself.*

July:

Therapist: *So you have to think . . . what kind of person do you want to be?*

July:

Therapist: *July?*

July: *I don't want to be a person.*

Therapist: *I understand what you're saying, but—*

July: *I. Don't. Want. To be.*

109.

now

When I wake up, the light is late. We have slept through most of the day. The last day. Panic floods me, and I know we have to go and see if anyone answered on the marquee. I try to pick up Yolo, and he hisses at me—which he never does—and turns his back. *I am cozy and want to sleep,* he is saying. *I kept watch with you last night and I'm tired.*

"I'm sorry, bud," I say. "We have to keep going."

Yolo doesn't move.

"Come with me?" I ask. "I think we're near the end. You can sit in the front seat."

Yolo glances over his shoulder at me and glares. I can read him clear as day. *Do not put that harness on me. Do not haul me around in a freaking cat backpack. Let me rest.*

"Okay." I tuck the blankets around him and stroke his back until he starts purring and I know I'm forgiven. "You've been a champ, Yo. I'll see you soon."

110.

once

JULY

Hey, the bonfire is coming up.

SYD

what bonfire

JULY

You know how on the last Friday of the summer the cross-country teams have a big team bonfire at Lakeside Park

the girls' captains are in charge of it this year since the guys did it last year

I already reserved one of the firepits and a pavilion earlier in the summer because they fill up fast

you have to be eighteen to do it but my mom did it for me

so that's all set

but we still have to decide what we're going to do there, all of that, talk to Alex, whatever

remember last year the team captains had us learn that cheesy song?

SYD

SYD

I was teasing you about not
remembering the bonfire

of COURSE I remember the freaking
bonfire

oh my gosh, MOM

JULY

whoops, sorry

so what do you think we should do?

SYD

way ahead of you there

I've got it all under control

111.

now

The minute I step out of my car, I can see they haven't written anything back. There's nothing added to the marquee.

Disappointment hits me in my heart, in my knees. I have to hold on to something to catch myself, and I lean on the rearview mirror, which creaks under my weight. So after a second I straighten up, tell myself to *be strong. Be smart.*

It still says 8/31 and GET TH3M BACK.

My IM SORRY letters have mostly blown away or fallen off. The O and the two *R*s are still standing.

The ladder is exactly where I left it after I fell.

But there's nothing new.

Wait. There's something at the *bottom* of the sign. Glistening in the late-afternoon sun of today.

Of 8/31.

It's the marquee letters that I couldn't find in the student government room. Scattered like leaves all around the base of the marquee.

And something else.

Propped up against the bottom of the marquee is a cross.

It's simple, plain, made of two sticks tied together with twine.

Pain hits me in my stomach, my hands, my feet. My whole body is pins and needles and knowing and recognition.

I have seen crosses like this before.

At the jump.

112.

once

"Summer's almost over," Sam said.

We were lying on a blanket underneath a tree outside of the Howell University library. On our way over from Sam's dorm room, a guy had called out to Sam by name as we walked by ("He's from freshman orientation," Sam had explained), and some girls—laughing, short-shorted—checked him out as they passed us on the sidewalk.

The campus that had been ours was now everyone's. Freshmen were everywhere; others were coming back. The excitement was palpable. Someone started singing the Howell University fight song and a bunch of people joined in, dissolving into laughter when they messed up at the end.

"It is." I smiled at him. Up close, his eyes had those gold flecks in them. In the distance, I heard music. A band somewhere else on campus for a welcome event, probably.

"I've been thinking a lot," Sam said. He wasn't smiling. And there was something in his voice I didn't like.

"Thinking a lot about what?" I asked.

"About us." The something was still there. It was getting worse, in fact.

"Oh yeah?" I rolled over on my stomach so I didn't have

to look at him. The evening air was warm, but when I reached down to pick a blade of grass, the ground was cool.

"Yeah," he said. I still didn't look at him. I found I couldn't. "July," he said, very soft. "You know how much I care about you."

And there it was. And there we were. I had felt it coming for me all summer. College guys don't date high school girls. No matter how much they like them. It always ends with the summer.

Even us.

He was breaking up with me.

I wanted to head him off.

I knew Sam was about to hurt me. I wanted to hurt him first.

"You know what *verity* means, right?" I sat up. Everywhere, people were laughing. Everywhere, night was about to come down.

"July," he said again.

"Answer the question." My voice was hard. I'd never talked to him like this before. But he'd earned it. "Do you know what *verity* means?"

He sat up, too.

"It's the name of the first owner's daughter," he said. His voice was gentle, perplexed. *He's humoring me,* I thought, and the pain of that, the humiliation of it, made me know this was really happening. He could humor me because I was no longer someone who mattered to him. He was placating me like a child, not fighting with me like a girlfriend. "They have that whole sign about it near the door. When he started the business back in the 1930s, he named it after her."

"You're right." I looked at him then. Right in the eyes. Neither of us flinched. "But it's not only a name, Sam. It's a name that is actually a word. Like Hope. Or Faith." Sam had always said that I was smart. That he liked that. But he hadn't liked it enough, had he? He hadn't liked *me* enough. "Did you know that?"

"No," he said.

"So," I said. "You don't actually know what *verity* means."

"I guess I don't." His voice was gentle.

"Truth," I said. "*Verity* means truth."

Sam was silent.

"So," I said. "Tell me the truth. You're about to break up with me, aren't you?"

"I'm sorry," he said. "I like you." He looked me straight in the eyes, his voice gentle. "I think I love you, even."

"What the hell, Sam?" I said. I wasn't sure what to do with my body. I had that feeling I always got when I needed to *move*. Like when I was sitting in class for too long, or in church, or when something was happening that made my brain tell me *we have to go*. I wanted to run and I couldn't. I stood up and folded my arms across my chest instead. "You're breaking up with me and you're also telling me that you love me for the first time?"

Sam stood up, too. He was looking at me, begging me to understand, but I didn't. At all.

"It's just that—" Sam stopped.

"What?" I said. "Say it."

Sam shook his head. "You know how when you're with

someone, and someone else asks you about them, you say, like, *she's really hot*. Or *she's really fun*. Or really smart, or cool, or whatever. With you I can't do that."

"Why not?" Was he telling me he didn't think I was any of those things?

"Because you're just . . . really."

"Really *what*?"

"Really everything."

I exhaled in frustration. I could feel tears burning behind my eyelids. "I don't understand."

"Remember when I told you you were dangerous?" he asked. "I didn't mean that you did dangerous stuff. Although you do. You guys play with fire all the time at the jump. I meant—" He swallowed, spoke again. "I meant that you are dangerous *for me*. I'm here to be in college. I'm here to have fun and learn and figure out who I am. I'm not here to fall crazy in love with someone."

"You're not crazy in love with me," I said. "If you were, you wouldn't be doing this." I took a step away. I couldn't hold still much longer.

"Where are you going?"

"Somewhere else," I said.

"Can I drive you there?"

"No."

He reached out for me, like he wanted to pull me into a hug, and I could not go there even though it was the place in the world I most wanted to be. It wasn't safe now. I took another step away from him.

"You didn't want to fall in love with me," I said. "So why did you?"

"I couldn't help it."

"You should have tried harder," I said, and I walked away. Before long, I was running.

113.

now

I kneel down in front of the cross.

My hands are shaking as I reach out to touch it.

Scattered all around like fallen plastic petals, the other marquee letters spell out nothing. They are a mess, some letters upside down, others flipped over the wrong way.

But it doesn't matter.

All I really have to say

All I've ever had to say

All I can say

Is what I've already said.

Over and over again.

Again.

I'M SORRY.

But those words have never been good enough.

And neither have I.

114.

once

Alex and I were sitting on his porch swing. I'd gone to his house after I'd left Sam. I didn't even know if Alex would be home. I didn't text first. He might have been with Syd. I don't know why I didn't go to her house first. I just didn't.

I knew I had to talk to someone.

I'd been in luck. Alex was home, and he came right out when he saw me. His dog Bo followed him outside and sat on my feet the way he always did. It meant we could never actually swing on the porch swing.

"Sam broke up with me," I said.

Alex started laughing.

I was shocked. Stung. I pushed against the ground, sending the swing into motion. Bo jumped up, betrayed. His expression said *This isn't how we do things.*

I know, I wanted to say to him. *It's not.*

"It's not funny."

"I know." Alex's voice went serious, his eyes sober. "I'm sorry."

"Then why are you laughing at me?" Nothing was making sense. Sam was in love with me but wanted to break up. Syd seemed to be pulling away from me. Alex was my best friend and he'd laughed in my face.

"It's like that old nineties song," Alex said. "You know? It has that chorus that says 'Everyone here, knows everyone here is thinking 'bout somebody else.' "

"Wow, Alex," I said. Now *I* was laughing, a hysterical edge to my voice. "I get the hint. Go be with Syd." I stood, but he stayed seated, looking up at me.

"It's all a mess," Alex said. "You want to be with Sam. Syd wants to be with Sam, and I want to be with you."

Wait.

What?

Syd wanted to be with *Sam?*

Alex wanted to be with *me?*

He didn't move. His eyes were locked on mine and his elbows were resting on his knees. And then he bit his lip. It felt like there was no safe place to look.

"I want to be with you." He said it again.

Emotional exhaustion and the headache that was slowly creeping up on me were making me stupid. I didn't know what to say. I didn't know what to want. "We already dated," I reminded him. "Back when we were sophomores."

"I don't think that counts." He took a deep breath. "I think we should give it another shot. What did we know back then?"

"Nothing," I agreed, but then I saw his eyes light up and I didn't want him to think this could happen. Because we were best friends. Because Syd had a crush on *him*, not Sam. Right? Because *I* was still in love with Sam. There was no way it could work.

"Exactly," he said.

"But we kissed," I said. "Remember?"

"Of course I remember," he said.

He didn't stand up. I didn't sit down.

"You didn't think it worked?"

"I mean, it did," I said. "The kiss did. But it only happened once."

"Ever since then." He stopped. Started. "Ever since then, I've wondered what it would be like if it happened again."

"They why haven't you said anything?"

"Because you were with Sam."

It was so ridiculous. I was on the edge of crying. "Alex," I said. "*You* broke up with *me* back then. And I wasn't with Sam until this summer. Why didn't you say anything before now?" I took a shaky breath. "You only realized you wanted me when I was with someone else."

Alex didn't say anything. He stood up.

It was too late.

115.

now

"I'm back," I call to Yolo, closing the door of the house behind me. "It's you and me, buddy. That's all I need. Just us. We don't have to do this anymore. We're done."

Downstairs, Yolo's food in his gray ceramic cat bowl is untouched. The water bowl is still full as well. He must not have come downstairs yet. "I should have stayed here, too," I call out. "Come on down and eat." I wait to hear his padding feet, his claws clicking on the hardwood. Nothing.

Where is he?

116.

now

When I left, I made sure everything was sealed up tight. Didn't I? I swear I did. But I was hurt and tired, and maybe I made a mistake?

What was I thinking, leaving him for even a minute?

There's his harness. I do remember taking that off when we came back earlier, because it would be ridiculous to tie Yolo up inside his own house.

I've assumed that the someone else in town is someone I want back, or someone who, on some level, might care about me.

But what if that's not the case?

Maybe Yolo's out catting around.

Hanging out with other cats, chasing small animals. But there haven't been any here since the Rapture. At least, not that I've seen.

Did something chase him?

Did someone *take* him?

Uneasiness catches at my heels as I spring up the stairs.

"Don't worry, Yo," I call out. "I'm coming."

117.

now

There's a shatter of glass in the bathroom.

A baseball bat in the middle of the floor. It's Jack's, the one I've been carrying around with me sometimes. I thought I'd left it in the car.

The space under the vanity, with no Yolo curled up underneath it. Only the blanket, and the other things I'd left there.

There's blood, a smear of it, on the grip of the bat.

Whoever swung the bat at the mirror did it with such force that the point of impact is perfectly preserved, a star-shaped imprint with shards radiating outward. It reminds me of how the water looks after you jump in—the circle, the ripples out.

Some of the fragments are on the floor.

They seem to be in a pattern. The shards laid end-to-end, spelling out . . .

GET THEM BACK.

118.

now

"Yolo?" I scream.

Yolo's not anywhere in my yard.

You found him before, remember? I tell myself. And, *He's a cat, of course he's going to find ways to do his own thing.* Yolo has stayed by my side a lot since he came back, even before I became a paranoid disaster and got the cat backpack and all that, but before all of this he always had a whole secret life I didn't know about.

He would wander off during the day or at night, come back ravenous or a bit disheveled, too cool to even meet your gaze when you fawned over him, so glad for his return. So maybe he's gone to one of those places that I've never known about. "This is Yolo's neighborhood, we just live in it," our neighbor had said once, and we'd laughed because it was so true.

My gaze must have flickered over to the fence between our yards, because that's when my eye catches on something. I walk closer to make sure.

Wait. There's Yolo's collar. Green to match his eyes, the kind that breaks away if it gets caught on anything.

It's snagged at the top of the fence. This has happened before, more than once. I walk over to pick it up. Yes. His. Green collar, silver tag, his name engraved on the front, our phone number on the back.

Sometimes I swear he breaks out of his collar on purpose.

"Yolo?" I call out. "YOLO!"

It's quiet.

The leaves rustle in the bushes near me. But it's only the wind, which settles as soon as it started. I kneel down to look for him anyway. Nothing.

There are no other cats for me to mistake for him. There aren't any small creatures crawling through the underbrush, giving me misguided hope.

"Do you know where he is?" I ask into the quiet.

No one I wished for would have taken him.

But I don't know who else is here.

119.

now

Okay. Okay. Where have Yolo and I gone together, both before and after this all happened? Is there somewhere he might have liked to try out without me?

Or *did* someone take him?

Maybe they do feel like I cheated. Maybe I have to go where they want me to go.

Because I've known all along where this ends.

I've been pretending there's a way to get out of it. To go to the marquee instead, to pretend that it could all end there, that I could get answers to my questions. But there are no answers.

That cross at the base of the sign.

I've known the whole time where the clues were going to lead me.

"No," I say out loud. *"No."*

I can't go *there.*

Not even for Yolo.

120.

now

I am losing the day. The hours are leaving.

It's going to rain. It's coming fast. The wind is whipping my hair. Leaves are flapping silver-gold above me, and the sky has gone almost-night dark.

"Yolo!" I call out, one more time. The collar dangles from my hand. Did he lose it going over into the neighbors' property, or coming back?

All I had to do was keep track of him . . .

All I had to do was keep him safe.

I know from before that you can try and try and try to re-construct what happened, and you can maybe get close, but you will never know.

And all you have are those words that give no comfort at all.

An accident.

It can be an accident, and you can still be to blame.

All I had to do was keep an eye on him. Just pay attention to the one living thing who loved me, and I failed.

Your fault your fault your fault.

Your fault your fault your fault.

Your fault this happened.

Your. Fault.

I look across the backyard.

And then I see.

121.

now

He is walking back across the yard to me, sleek and free.

122.

now

"Hey," I say. I reach for him, and he darts away. He sees the collar dangling in my hand.

"You have to wear this," I say. Tears are streaming down my face, and my throat is hoarse from calling out for him. "The tag says your name. What number to call if you get lost. Who you belong to."

I have owned him since my ninth birthday, for over nine years now.

I have never owned him.

You can never own anything that is alive, at all.

123.

now

I walk over to the trash can in the backyard and throw in the collar. Yolo watches me from under our picnic table, where he has taken cover from the rain.

124.

now

When I sit down on the back porch steps, Yolo comes over to me. He climbs on my lap, and when I pat his back, his coat is dirty and wet. He has been out adventuring and hasn't had time to clean it yet.

"There, there," I say, as I run my hand along his back. I don't sing to him this time. "There, there. You'll be okay."

He looks up at me as if to say, *I know. I've always been okay. Except when you put me in that stupid backpack.*

And drove me all over town when you already know where you have to go.

It's true.

I didn't go where I always knew I had to go, where all the clues were leading me, because I didn't want to go there. I didn't want anything bad to happen. I didn't want to repeat the mistakes of this night a year ago. The mistakes I've made ever since.

Yolo jumps off my lap. Has he heard something stirring in the bushes? Or is it only the wind, the rain? Either way, he wants to go.

"Okay," I say. "Okay."

He looks back at me, one glance, quick-fast.

And then he is gone.

I reach over my shoulder, put my hand on my back. "There, there," I say to myself, my knees dirty from kneeling on the ground to look for Yolo, my own hand leaving a print on my own shirt.

There.

There.

125.

now

GET TH3M BACK.

It's been written so many places now.

In my journal, on the marquee. On the side of the dugout, with the glass shards here in the bathroom, where I've come to gather my things.

"Get you back," I say. "Okay."

Maybe I will.

I feel angry.

I like it.

It has been a long time since I felt this.

I *will* get you back.

For everything.

126.

Therapist: *There is a quote that I'd like to share with you. It has to do with what we've been talking about. Mindfulness, and impermanence.*

July: *Okay.*

Therapist: *It's from a monk named Thich Nhat Hanh. Would it be all right if I read it to you?*

July:

July: *Okay.*

Therapist: *"Living is a joy. Dying in order to begin again is also a joy. Starting over is a wonderful thing, and we are starting over constantly."*

July:

Therapist: *Did that quote mean anything to you? Or speak to you in any way? It doesn't have to.*

July:

Therapist: *July, where are you going?*

127.

now

I know what I have to do.

I place the items—one, two, three, four, five; sticker, baseball, bucket, napkin, cross—into the backpack I used for Yolo. I pull it on over my shoulders. All the clues are inside. Except for the journal, which I burned.

And the running shoes, which I carry with me to the front porch steps. I pull the shoes on over my feet. I make sure the laces are tied tight.

Once they are, I stand up and stretch. My arms and legs, my quads and calves. I crouch as if someone is going to fire a gun, legs taut, arms at the ready, and then

I whisper to myself

go.

128.

once

The Fall Creek Girls Manifesto

We are the Fall Creek Girls.

We travel in a pack.

We run faster than fast, harder than hard.

Our feet push off the ground. Blood pumps in our veins and pounds in our hearts.

We know how to tear up a hill and how to fly past you when we're tired. We're not immortal, but we're as close as anyone can be.

When we're together, we turn heads. People pause, they watch, they look.

We make people jealous.

Older people wish their bodies worked like ours.

Little kids wish they were us. They want our long legs. Our laughter. Our freedom. Our arms draped over each other's shoulders, our ponytails swinging when we walk.

We run all over town, but there is one run in particular that defines us.

It starts in a gorge that could break you. It doesn't break us. We run up the stone steps, through the crevice the water has cut. Across the suspension bridge, a thread over the gorge. It is secret and misty in early mornings. We go down a long road, past Flatrock. The sun chases us along that road and through green farmland, rolling hills. Then we cut through the wildflower preserve, through the grass and blossoms and rumbling bees, to Fall Creek, where the water is deep and emerald green and the cliffs are darkest gray.

You can live a lifetime in a long run.

This one ends at the jump.

129.

now

The rain is rolling back as the sun lowers in the sky. It's like the world, the town, nature, whatever is in charge, is saying *Good. You got the message. You're doing what we asked. You're going where you know you have to go.*

Was there ever any other choice?

Moving on, moving on. Everyone is moving on.

Except me.

I'm stuck here.

I know who I wished for.

We have *to have this,* my heart said.

But we will not survive it, my head answered.

Both right.

I was scared of impermanence, of change and loss. But this—this me alone, nothing changing, no one left to lose—this is unbearable. I know what I have to do.

I can't stay here anymore.

And there is only one way to leave.

I begin with the gorge that could break you.

130.

once, that night

what time do you need me there to
help set up for the bonfire?

SYD

Alex and I have it covered

just come whenever

we've got it all figured out

all you have to do is show up

131.

now

In the gorge, you can see the layers of stone made over time. You can reach out and touch them.

You have layers over layers of memories in a place. There is the deepest layer, with the ones you love the most, or have the most memories with. Years and years and years. *Maybe,* you think, *I'll make new memories here with new people.* Because you can't give up the place entirely—it's physically impossible, or emotionally.

And there you are, and both you and the place are layered, like wallpaper on top of wallpaper for centuries, and you'd have to peel everything away, you'd have to be the bare boards, no memories, nothing left. To get rid of some things, you'd have to get rid of everything.

So then you are. There you are. Living on.

A house with ghosts.

132.

once, that night

ELLA

could I get a ride to the bonfire
tonight?

JULY

sure. I might have to stay late to
help out because I'm one of the team
captains, okay?

ELLA

yes of course

I'm sorry.

JULY

No worries. Happy to give you a ride

ELLA

no, I mean I'm sorry I didn't jump
today

JULY

nothing to be sorry about

you can jump when you're ready, or
not at all

it's not a thing, I promise

ELLA

It is a thing

JULY

It's okay. I promise.

ELLA

but this was the last Friday of the
summer

This was my last chance

JULY

It's not your last chance

Everything's going to be okay.

133.

now

The stairs along the gorge are cut out of stone and are slate-gray, dark and slick where the rain has hit them, where it creeps through the earth. They line the gorge, the creek falling away below them.

There are so many edges in this town.

The edge of your heart, where it tore when someone left or walked away. The edge of your mind, when you feel it slipping dark. The edges of the things that should never have been said. The ones that cut and you can't take back.

I was wrong, I realize, *when I thought I didn't have to keep running. I do.*

I always, always do.

134.

once, that night

We pulled into the parking lot by one of the pavilions in Lakeside Park. I could see the red-and-white lights of Verity Ice Cream a couple of blocks away. In the opposite direction, closer to the lake, the bonfire was already going. Music played from a speaker set up on one of the picnic tables.

I waved at Alex, who was near the fire, stacking wood. He nodded at me, his hands busy. Coolness and a deep, watery scent came off the lake. "I'll meet up with you in a few minutes, okay?" I said to Ella, and she nodded. Morgan was already calling her over.

I headed for the pavilion, where Syd was cueing up music on her phone. "Hey," she said. Her blond hair was loose, cascading down her back and glinting in the light. I saw her look past me for a moment, and I turned to see Alex still working on the fire, a bunch of guys gathering around him.

"Thanks for taking care of all this," I said, trying to keep the hurt out of my voice. I didn't want to get mad at her for arranging things without me. And I understood that she might have wanted a chance to hang out with Alex. An extra reason. Plus, I'd been preoccupied with Sam. First with being with him, then with losing him.

Plus, what was I supposed to do about what Alex had said?

"No problem." Syd's voice sounded flat, like it had that day I brought lunch to the river for her and Alex.

"What can I do now?"

"Alex is building the bonfire, and I'm in charge of the music," she said. Then Syd's eyes came to life, sparked with an idea, looked more like the Syd I loved. "Actually, can you read the manifesto when we get started? We're going to do that instead of teaching them a song or whatever."

"What about the guys?" I asked. "The manifesto's not really for them."

"It'll be fine," Syd said. "Alex has something planned for them."

"Okay," I said. "But I didn't bring a copy of it."

"I've got one left in my car," Syd said. "In the glove compartment." She tossed me her keys.

"Awesome." I lingered, but there wasn't anything else.

"That's it," she said, cheerfully. Was it just me, or were we still disconnected? We'd texted about the breakup with Sam, sure, but this was the first time we'd seen each other in person. Didn't she want to give me a hug? Ask me how I was doing? I wanted her to do that.

And I wanted to ask her, *Why have we been off lately?*
What have I done or not done?
Who can I be, or not be, to get you to love me again?

135.

now

Again, I have the sense of someone just ahead of me, disappearing around a corner before I do.

"*Syd,*" I whisper. "*Alex. Sam. Ella. Jack. Mom. Dad.*" There are other names I could say. Who else is out there?

I've almost finished the climb up through the gorge. My heart pounds, my quads scream with exertion, my calves are wire tight.

Are these leaves moving because someone brushed past them moments ago? Someone light as air, fast as the wind, hiding from me? Someone who knows everything, and exactly what clues to leave and actions to take to pull me along. To take me where I don't want to go.

Who is it?

I think I might know.

I hope I do.

I hope I don't.

Wait, I think. *Wait for me.*

Out loud, I say, "I'm right behind you."

136.

once, that night

I unlocked Syd's car. We hardly ever rode in it, but I knew the watermelon smell.

Hardly ever rode in it *together*, that was. It seemed she'd been driving around to deliver the manifestos on her own. No apple stickers on *her* glove compartment, of course. I popped it open. Inside, the last manifesto, rolled up and secured with a blue-and-gold hair tie.

I didn't have Sam anymore.

I wasn't sure about Syd, about Alex.

But I still had my team.

137.

now

Over the suspension bridge hanging above the creek, the wooden slats and ropes swinging with the momentum of my run. The water underneath is shallow, even after the rain.

The rocks beneath are slick and flat and hard.

You don't have to fall far to break. You need almost no water at all to drown.

138.

once, that night

On my way back, I could see that everyone had begun milling around the bonfire in the lowering light. When Syd saw me, she called out, "Okay, everyone! Gather around! July's got something for the girls' team. And then Alex has something planned for the guys."

She had dragged a picnic table near the bonfire and was climbing to stand on top. The girls gathered around, the boys behind them. "Come on," she called to me, and I climbed up on the table next to her. The ground in the park wasn't even, it was hillocky and patchy in places, and so the table felt unsteady.

Once I was next to Syd, she motioned for everyone to be quiet. After a second or two, they were. They remembered the beginning of the summer, when we were playing night games and she'd showed them she meant business by low-key humiliating that kid. Now we knew him—his name was Rowan Sharp, he was funny and medium fast, we'd joked around with him near the Gatorade cooler Coach Warren always brought to practice.

We all knew each other now. Didn't we?

"Okay, everyone," Syd said. "By now you all know that we have a lot of traditions. Some of them have been around for a while, like the bonfire and the jump. They're part of who we are." She gestured to me. "July's going to read something. It's called the Fall Creek Girls Manifesto. Once you're one of us, that doesn't end with high school. It goes on forever." She motioned for me to go ahead and climbed down from the picnic table so that I was up there alone.

The fire snapped showers of sparks. The sky was nearing navy-blue dark.

Everyone was quiet.

I began to read.

We are the Fall Creek Girls.

We travel in a pack.

We run faster than fast, harder than hard.

Our feet push off the ground. Blood pumps in our veins and pounds in our hearts.

We know how to tear up a hill and how to fly past you when we're tired. We're not immortal, but we're as close as anyone can be.

When we're together, we turn heads. People pause, they watch, they look.

We make people jealous.

Older people wish their bodies worked like ours.

Little kids wish they were us. They want our long legs. Our laughter. Our freedom. Our arms draped over each other's shoulders, our ponytails swinging when we walk.

We run all over town, but there is one run in particular that defines us.

It starts in a gorge that could break you. It doesn't break us. We run up the stone steps, through the crevice the water has cut. Across the suspension bridge, a thread over the gorge. It is secret and misty in early mornings. We go down a long road, past Flatrock. The sun chases us along that road and through green farmland, rolling hills. Then we cut through the wildflower preserve, through the grass and blossoms and rumbling bees, to Fall Creek, where the water is deep and emerald green and the cliffs are darkest gray.

You can live a lifetime in a long run.

This one ends at the jump.

As I read it, the girls joined in, almost chanting. They knew all the lines. Syd must have told them to memorize it. They sounded powerful, saying the words that I'd written. Saying the words that we were.

As we finished the last few lines, I noticed something I hadn't before. They were all wearing their hair ties.

Except Ella.

And her lips weren't moving.

Because she didn't know the words.

She hadn't jumped.

139.

now

Down, down the long, quiet Fall Creek Road, the green trees forming almost a tunnel, a cocoon, overheard. Now that I am on my way, the rain has gone, the sun is setting. Evening gold through green, not the same as morning gold through the same trees. If you have been out in both, you know the difference.

I hear the water of the creek to my left as it makes its way over the stones at Flatrock. On both sides, the big trees and old homes keep watch over the road, over all the things and people that have passed along it all these years.

Now everyone is gone.

140.

once, that night

Ella's eyes were huge.

She knew this wasn't my idea. Didn't she?

But *I* was the one holding the manifesto in my hand. The hair tie was on *my* wrist.

These were my words. I wasn't going to let Syd change what I'd meant by them. This was my team, too.

I could still fix this.

"And while I'm up here," I said, "we want to recognize our fastest freshman—someone who might turn out to be our fastest runner, in fact—as part of the team." I didn't look at Syd. I held out the manifesto in one hand, the hair tie in the other. "Ella Kane, would you please come up?"

The guys and girls started cheering. Ella came forward, head ducked, but when she looked up at me, her eyes were shining.

She said something I couldn't hear as she took the manifesto and hair tie from me.

141.

now

At this point in the run, you're heading back toward town, but in a different way from the way you came out. This is not an out-and-back. This is a loop.

A loop with a break, at the cliffs and the jump, before going on down back to the high school, near the lake.

I am on the return.

142.

once, that night

"What the hell was that?" Syd asked.

"I could ask you the same thing." I folded my arms across my chest.

"You gave Ella the manifesto!" Syd said. "She's not supposed to get that until she jumps."

"I never agreed to that," I said.

"You knew it was happening that way, and you never said anything until now."

"I didn't feel like I could."

Syd scoffed. "Okay. Still. Then you singled her out to be special."

"*You* were the one singling her out!" I said. "Didn't you see her face?"

"I thought you had my back," Syd said.

"I do—"

She shook her head. "We did everything together. Everything. We shared our clothes. You knew the freaking password to my phone. I always had *your* back."

"And I've always had yours," I said. Why was she speaking in past tense? Was she mad about the manifesto thing, or something else? Alex?

"I'm sorry I came to Flatrock that day with you and Alex."

Maybe that whole misunderstanding had been the problem. Had she been waiting all this time for me to apologize? I'd thought we were past it.

"That's not it." Syd turned around. Her face was hard, but behind it I thought I could see pain.

Then what *was* it?

"I know I spent most of my time with Sam this summer. Too much." My words were tumbling on top of one another. I had to say them fast enough. If I found the right ones, I could say them, and if I could say them, I could fix this. "And I'm sorry I wasn't very helpful with planning the bonfire."

Syd shook her head. "That isn't it, either."

"Then *tell* me!" I said. "I know I haven't been perfect. But you're right. You've always had my back. And I've always tried to have yours."

"Right."

"I'm serious!" I was shaking with the unfairness of it all.

"Did you tell Alex I liked him?"

"No, I swear."

Syd shook her head. "You couldn't even do *that* for me. You are *so* damn selfish."

I felt like I kept blundering into different traps. "I thought you didn't want me to!" Wasn't that what she'd said the last time we talked about it?

"*Stop.*" Syd took a deep breath. "You don't get it." A breeze was coming off the lake, teasing tendrils of hair out from her ponytail. Her eyes were inscrutable, closed-off.

"Are you breaking up with me?" I asked, trying to make a joke out of it. What was happening? My voice sounded high, stressed out, embarrassing. I tried again. "Syd. Seriously. Is something wrong?"

"Nothing's wrong."

Behind us, someone threw another log onto the bonfire. The sparks flew up and crackled; I could hear them, but I didn't turn to see. I kept my eyes on Syd, on her face in the flickering firelight. Were we okay? Was this going to be okay? I couldn't lose her, too.

"So did *you* ever talk to Alex?" I asked. Trying to fill that crackling silence.

She laughed once, bright. When Syd was feeling a lot of emotion, she didn't get messy or stumble over her words. She became uber-precise, each syllable clipped and careful. "I did. He told me he's into someone else."

I felt the air leave my lungs.

"What?" I asked. "Wait." My heart sank. And then—it soared. Did that mean . . .

"So," Syd said conversationally. "That's fun."

"Syd," I said. "I didn't—I don't—" My mind was whirling.

She cut me off. "No worries." She'd turned away. I couldn't see her well in the dark. Was she crying?

All summer Syd and I had been breaking. But I didn't know for sure we were fully broken, like, for good, until that night at the lake, when the bonfire licked the sky and the lake licked the shore and everything unraveled.

I missed her. I missed her so much. We used to do everything together. Eat lunch together, go on walks together, see movies together; find each other every minute we were alone so that we were never lonely.

I didn't know if I missed her or Sam more, in that moment. They both felt so very, very far gone.

"Hey," I said, and I put my hand on Syd's arm. She moved so we were no longer touching. She still wasn't looking at me.

"It doesn't even matter, you know," she said.

"What doesn't?"

"Giving the manifesto to Ella. Everyone still knows she didn't jump." There was something smiling and cold in her voice. "Especially Ella."

She turned on her heel and walked off toward the bonfire, so fast I'd have had to run to catch her. And I was too tired to do it. I was sick of chasing, of running races other people had set for me.

All summer long, we'd been in the water.

Now everything was going up in flames.

143.

now

The backpack bounces between my shoulder blades. The bucket and baseball clunk against each other. The Verity napkin's likely getting crushed, crumpled. Probably the apple sticker is stuck to something else in there. I hope the cross doesn't break.

I've been missing them for what feels like forever. Carrying them around with me when everyone else was moving on.
Except me.
I'm stuck here.
I have to break free.
Even if it means
that I have to do
this.

144.

once, that night

"Hey," I said to Alex. I'd been waiting for a moment when he wasn't talking to anyone. People were gathering in smaller groups, and the bonfire was in full blaze, logs snapping, the flames high enough that I wondered if the police would come by and give us a warning.

Alex and I separated ourselves from the others. His hair was wild and I wished he would hug me. Like he had so many times before. I felt an ache where I'd always pictured my heart being as a kid. Right in the center of my chest under my breastbone.

"What was going on there?" Alex asked. "With Syd and the manifesto thing and all that?"

"It's a long story." I felt jittery, and my heart was pounding so hard I could feel it in my throat, my wrists. I was about to do something crazy. Why not?

"Is Ella okay?" he asked.

"Yeah, I think so." I didn't look to see where she was. All night I'd been paying attention to how everyone else felt. Now I was going to think about what I wanted to do. What I needed. I'd been trying to do the right thing for everyone else, and I kept on screwing it up. I kept on managing to not do what they wanted at all.

"Swing?" I asked him.

"Okay," he said.

We walked over to the park swings. They were the durable kind, heavy chain-link with blue plastic seats. Deep grooves were worn into the grass beneath them, and goose droppings littered the ground.

"I always forget how much bird crap there is here," I said.

"Me too."

We sat down next to each other and pushed away from the ground and up into the air. "I'm winning," I said, when I got higher faster, and then we were totally in sync for a couple of back-and-forths. In the rush of the muggy lake-scented air, I lost track of the sounds of the bonfire crackling and people talking behind us. It was me and Alex, our legs dangling in the sky, and that was all.

"We should go back," Alex said a few minutes later, as we slowed, stopped.

"Yeah."

He looked at me.

Now or never. It was like making the jump for the first time. I had thought about it so many times. And now I was going to go off the edge. Adrenaline prickled through me in a rush.

I'm going over.

"Let's try it," I said. "Let's go out."

"Wait," Alex said. *"What?"*

"Why not?" I asked.

He turned in his swing so we were looking directly at each other. I couldn't quite read his expression. "You just broke up with Sam."

"Well, he broke up with me," I said. "Technically." I laughed.

It sounded giddy and shaky to my own ears. "Still." I wasn't quite sure what was happening. It hadn't even been a week ago that Alex had suggested this exact thing, and I'd said no. So why wasn't he happy? Why wasn't he jumping at this?

"I can't."

"Why not?" I was stunned. He'd wanted this, earlier. And Syd had been talking about me and Alex, hadn't she? *He told me he's into someone else.* That's what she had said, literally minutes ago.

"I can't."

He couldn't even give me a reason? All these years and shared moments? All the ice cream eaten and races run and mini-golf games played and talks at night, and he couldn't even give me a reason?

"I'm not there anymore," Alex said. He stood up, the swing chain jangling slightly. "I've moved on."

I started to laugh. I couldn't help it. I stood up, too, wishing I weren't laughing, desperate to close the gap I felt growing between us. "Wait. It's only been a few days. You changed your mind that fast?"

"It hasn't been days for me," he said. "It's been years. I was there for a long time, and now I'm not."

"But we didn't even get through all the ice cream flavors," I told Alex stupidly.

"I know."

"Do you think you might go back?" I tried to say it funny. Without crying. "To where you were?" But my voice broke. The way Alex looked at me was not a way he had ever looked at me before.

"No," he said. "I can't."

We stood there, the two of us. There was everything and nothing left to say. *We almost made it,* I thought. *We almost made it to each other.*

145.

now

I have found my stride at last. My pace is steady and smooth. These roads are mine now.

Deep green fields stretch out in the lowering light, barns and fences rising up out of the farmland. The trees at the edges seem to be waiting to take back the land. *You played here for a few centuries,* they say, *but we will have it again.*

146.

once, that night

Ella found me at the edge of the lake. I seemed to have washed up there, the way dead fish and plastic wrappers and paper cups sometimes did. "Hey," she said. "July. Are you okay?"

"Yeah." The toes of my shoes were wet, and I knew if I took another step into the water, the mud would make a sucking sound. "Are you?"

The tears were coming silently. I wasn't making any noise, but they kept sliding down my cheeks, dripping off my chin.

"I'm okay," Ella said. "Thank you. For what you did. That was really—"

"I'm sorry," I said. I felt horrible interrupting her and at the same time I felt nothing doing it. "Can you find another ride home? I need to go."

"I'll come with you." Now Ella sounded like she might cry, too. Had she seen Syd and me fighting, or Alex and me on the swings, or heard that Sam and I had broken up? I heard something in her voice. Was she mad at me about the manifesto? Had I done the wrong thing there, too?

"I need to be alone," I said. "Please."

The air was full of bonfire sounds—people were talking, and someone, Syd maybe, had turned the speaker up—but I had never felt more alone.

"I'm sorry," Ella said.

"You don't have anything to apologize for," I said. "But I have to go. Now. By myself. You can get a ride with Syd. Or Alex. Okay?"

"Okay," she said. "But are you sure you're all right?"

"I'm fine." I wiped my eyes with the back of my hand.

"You're not," she said. "What can I do?" Ella put her hand on my shoulder. It was so gentle, so kind. It was the first time anyone had touched me since Sam and I had broken up.

And that undid me.

It's heartbreaking when someone actually, truly, deeply wants to be the right person for you. To be there for you. And they're a good person, and maybe they could be, could have been the right person, but *you* have become so wrong, such a wrong person, that it doesn't even matter anymore.

"I can't be your friend right now," I told Ella.

She looked like I'd slapped her in the face. Her hand dropped from my shoulder.

"Why?" she asked. "What did I do?"

"No, no," I told her. "It's nothing you've done."

"Is it because I didn't jump?"

"What?" I said. "No. It has nothing to do with that. And nothing to do with you. You're awesome."

"Okay," she said. Her eyes were wide. I could tell she was reeling, trying to understand. "Okay."

"You can still text me," I said. "I'll still give you rides. But that's all. Okay?"

I turned away before I could hear her answer.

I was trying to help.

I thought she would be better off if I wasn't around.

I know.

Believe me, I know. You could pave a road to hell with my good intentions.

It felt like it took forever to walk to my car, to climb inside and drive away.

I ruin everything, I thought.

But I never meant to ruin *her.*

147.

now

The farmland is strange without animals in it. The horse pastures are empty.

Long and lean and beautiful, the animals that used to live here, that used to race us and make us laugh. Because we knew we could never beat them, no matter how hard we tried.

148.

once, that night

I didn't get far. Two streets over, into the Verity parking lot. Through the door with the chime, to the register with the chalkboard menu up on the wall behind it.

"Hi," I said. "I'd like a scoop of peaches and cream." That was the flavor Alex and I had been up to eat next, before the summer went off the rails, before we missed each other and he said it couldn't change.

"Sure," Sam said. Our eyes locked before he looked away to pick up a scoop. There was a strain in his voice that no one else in line would likely have noticed but me.

He handed me the ice cream and looked near me but not at me as he rang me up. "There you go," he said.

"Thanks," I said.

I used to kiss along the line of your jaw and you used to catch your breath. You used to put your hands on my shoulders, wrap them around my waist, rest them on my hips.

I sat at a table out on the patio and ate my ice cream. It was delicious. *I think when you're depressed, you're supposed to not eat,* I thought. *You're supposed to be all faint and wan and heroin-chic.*

But I was so hungry.

Someone had left a printed copy of the ice cream flavor menu on the table. A corner of it was missing, and all of it was sticky.

Someone sat down across from me.

Sam.

"Hey," he said. "Are you okay?"

"I'm great," I said. The ice cream was slightly salty in my mouth because I was still crying.

"I'm sorry I haven't texted," he said. "I just felt like it was, you know, easier for both of us to move on."

"Totally," I said. "Good call."

"I thought maybe you came here because you wanted to talk to me," he said. "So I took my break. I'm on my break." He exhaled, looked at me. Not the way he'd looked at me at the cash register a few minutes ago. Straight on. In the eyes. He blinked.

"We broke up," I said.

"Yeah," he said.

"I didn't come here to talk to you," I said. That was a lie. I had. But when I saw he wouldn't even meet my eyes at the register, I knew. If someone won't look at you, you can't change anything. "I came here to eat ice cream."

I ate the last bite. I stood up to push my chair back. It suddenly felt critical that I leave, right now. Before I smiled at him or reached out to touch his hand or did any of the things I used to do that I couldn't anymore.

"This is actually my last night working here," Sam said, pushing his chair back, too. "I got a job at Howell. Working in the bookstore."

"That's great for you," I said. It didn't matter that Sam

wouldn't work at Verity anymore. I still wouldn't come back here again, because it would remind me of Alex, too.

"Thanks." Sam's voice was soft.

"You're welcome," I said. "Have a nice life."

It felt imperative that I walk away first.

So I did.

149.

now

On to the wildflower preserve, graceful with Queen Anne's lace and yarrow, all silvery-white now in the coming night, grays and whites of varying depths. The hills are covered in trees, and from the preserve, everything is so peaceful you have no idea of the creek, the cliffs, the spillway
   the edges
   waiting for you.

150.

once, that night

"I'm home," I said.

My voice shook.

No one answered.

There was a note on the counter from my parents.

At the Howards' for dinner.

I hoped that maybe Jack and his friends were in the family room playing video games like they often were. But when I headed down the hall, all I heard was silence. I should have known from the kitchen. No empty chip bags, no spills of soda on the counter. Yolo wasn't anywhere to be found. Everyone had somewhere else to be. No one had me.

I felt so *sad*. Like the ground had dissolved under my feet. Like I was reaching for a handhold and there was only air and so much space. If you can't even count on your family, what do you have left at all?

Mom. Dad. Jack.

Don't you even notice me slipping away?

Can't you see that glass is shattering all around me?

151.

now

The sun is setting. It's slow at first, the gold ebbing away almost imperceptibly, a filtering and loss so incremental you have just begun to notice it's going when suddenly

    it's all

    the way

    gone.

152.

once, that night

I was still standing alone in the family room of my house.

I was still standing.

My phone buzzed with a text. My heart leapt in spite of myself. Was someone reaching out? Did someone care? Syd? Sam? Alex?

Ella.

I'm sorry.

I know you said you couldn't be my friend.

But I had to tell you.

I'm going to do it.

Now.

For a second, I wasn't sure what she meant, but then it hit me like a baseball bat to the stomach, like a sharp shard of glass to my heart:

She's going to jump.

153.

now

I am almost through the wildflower preserve. Almost to the trees, their black shapes printed against a sky whose sun has just set.

Once, my therapist asked me, "What if you could sit down everyone you wanted to talk with, and ask them all the questions you're wanting to ask?"

That is what I have been doing in my mind, over and over again, since everyone disappeared. I've been asking them all the questions I never got to ask.

I know them all so well.

I don't know them at all.

Do you really know me?

Did I really know you?

If so

how could we let each other go?

154.

once, that night

I texted back *Wait*
  Wait for me
  Don't do it yet
  I'm on my way
    I had to find the keys had to find the keys where did I put
the keys
    I remembered what Syd had said
    about how *Ella* knew she still hadn't jumped.
    Syd was right.
    My giving Ella the manifesto—
    My telling her we couldn't be friends, after promising to
help her—
    All summer long, I'd felt like Syd was forcing Ella to jump
    and now it was me
    sending her over the edge.

155.

now

I hear the water pouring over the spillway and into the pool, a deep blue-black green in the just-fallen night. The last of the light glints off the water. At the top of the cliff, trees cling to the edges where the stone crumbles away.

I am almost at the jump.

156.

once, that night

I was driving too fast but everything finally felt crystal clear.

Screen-blue light seeped through windows. Kids were playing outside as the night came down. There was a snick-hiss of sprinklers coming on in some of the yards, and through my rolled-down window, I could smell burgers being grilled.

I passed other cars along the road. People out with their dogs. A woman opened the door of her house, carrying a plate of cookies, and walked across the yard to the house next door.

A man pushed his lawnmower into the garage.

There was a group of lanky middle schoolers talking by a mailbox at the curb, some kids gathered in the park at the end of the road, their parents watching.

There were people jogging along the road, teenagers walking together in knots on the sidewalk, students sprawled in the long grassy areas by the college dorms.

I still thought, *I can fix it.*

Not everything.

But one thing.

If I could just fix one thing, that would be enough to hold on to.

157.

now

There are three basic elements to this town, underneath everything else we've layered on top of it. Water, trees, stone. They are in different combinations, and sometimes one wins out over the others, but there are all three always there. For you to move with, come upon, break against.

I slow, make my way carefully through the forest. The light is going going almost gone.

I learned that night that the edges will come up on you.

158.

once, that night

I started running for the jump from the parking lot, breathless, the light going going almost gone. I cut through the trees, bushes scratching my shins in the dark. Closer. Closer. I was almost there, almost to the edge, when I came down wrong on a piece of uneven ground and twisted my ankle.

I swore out loud.

But it wasn't broken, and I could still walk, and so I stood up and started limping through the trees. Almost there. I took in a deep breath to call out, and that's when I heard them.

159.

now

I breathe in, out. In, out. Remembering.

The last time we came here together.

The last time we did *anything* together.

I didn't know it was the end, of course.

You never do.

I was trying to help. And I didn't. I kept trying trying to help trying trying to fix trying trying to go back to how it had been and I failed. I failed that night at the jump and so many other times, too.

But this time

it's okay.

I'm the only person

left to hurt.

160.

once, that night

I saw them. I knew their bodies. The lines of their faces when turned toward me, or away.

Ella was there.

And Alex.

He was holding her hand.

I stopped. They hadn't heard me.

They didn't even know I was there.

161.

now

I can feel the space opening up somewhere past the trees: the dark emptiness and fall of the jump, the smell of ancient stone and deep water.

And there below, the rocks.

162.

once, that night

"Oh," I said, out loud.

It was such a stupid thing to say.

I was such a stupid thing to be.

But they hadn't heard me. I wasn't quite loud enough.

"It was really nice what she did," Ella said. "Giving me the manifesto and everything."

"Yeah," Alex said. "It was."

"I guess she's not coming," Ella said. "I texted her."

"It's okay," Alex said. "I'll jump with you."

"Okay," she said, but neither of them moved. He took a step closer, but not to the water. To her. They were still holding hands.

163.

now

I remember something, a secret, about being in the dimness before the dark. If you're there
  long enough
  longer than you think you can stand,
  you remember:
  You were once an animal. Nothing but gut and instinct.
  And here's another secret.
  You can be one again.

164.

once, that night

I couldn't help anyone.
   No one needed me.
   There was nothing left to fix.
   There was no one left to text.
   And I wanted to push. Them.
   Right
   Over
   The edge.

165.

now

I shrug off the pack and take out each item.
    I line them up at the edge of the jump.
    An apple sticker.
    A baseball.
    A plastic berry bucket.
    A torn Verity napkin.
    The running shoes are still on my feet.
    Last of all, I take out the cross.

166.

once

I have a different story for you, my mother said once.

A different story about what?

About dying.

Mom, there's no other story. You were right. We die. That's it.

This is a story my dad told me that is also true. I just remembered it.

Can I tell it to you?

I didn't say anything.

She waited. Then, when she heard that my crying was slowing down, she started in.

My dad—your grandpa—said dying was like being called in from playing outside on a summer's night.

When you're little, and you hear your parents calling you, and you're out with your friends playing, or catching fireflies with your brother, or making nests for your stuffed animals out of the fresh-cut grass or kissing the person you like, you don't want to come in. You can't imagine ever wanting to come in.

But when you get older, and you're tired, and you're sitting on the porch, and you still love the stars but a lot of the people you love have already gone in, you don't mind as much. Maybe you hear someone you miss very much calling you. So when they do, you stand up. You take one last look at the stars. Your heart is very full.

And you go inside.

That's nice, I said to her. Really nice. But that assumes that people miss you. Or that you get to be old.

That assumes that you don't get called

or decide

to go in

way too soon.

167.

now

"I was there!" I scream. It echoes off the walls of the gorge, the stones sending it back. *I was there!* My voice breaks. *"I was with you!"*

Didn't it mean anything to them?

It had all meant everything to me.

My parents. Jack.

Alex. Syd. Sam. Ella.

They had all meant everything to me.

They still do.

Mistake upon mistake, all of them compounding and stratifying in layers, like the stones in the gorge. Wearing away like water at the people I loved, so that finally something came loose and it all washed away in a flood, in an instant.

It made me boundless, but not in a good way. I didn't seem to know who I was without the edges of other people to come up against.

A year ago tonight, someone broke at the jump.

once, that night

Ella and Alex were going to jump, together. They didn't need me anymore. Even though I'd tried to make things right. I'd apologized to Syd for whatever it was I'd done. I'd told Alex I wanted to be with him. I made sure Ella got the manifesto. You can do good things—for the right reasons, even—and still not be good enough.

I wasn't good enough. I never would be.

Syd had already been mad at me, and what I'd done at the bonfire had sent her over the edge.

Ella was going to jump.

And Alex would be with her.

They had each other. They did not need me.

No one

needed me.

I think I was crying, then.

I stepped back, away. My shoes on the dirt at the edge of the cliff.

I didn't want them to know I was there.

I didn't want them to reach out and draw me in. I didn't belong. Not there not anywhere not to anyone anywhere.

I stepped back, back, back.

Again.

169.

now

You think it's the sad memories that break you. The times they walked away, or hurt you so much that you turned away instead.

But it's the good ones that take you down. The big things they did to help you. The smallest things that made them who they are, made them who you still love in spite of everything they did and you did and the world did.

It's the times that were beautiful. That were so, so good.

You can never

get them back.

170

Syd, *in the rain, in the parking lot of the grocery store.*

Sam, in the water, in the dark.

Alex, laughing across the artificial green turf of the mini-golf course.

Ella, waiting in front of her house, holding her running shoes, beaming.

Mom, lifting piece after piece of shattered glass, tears in her eyes.

Dad, handing out tinfoil dinners by the fire.

Jack, swinging at the ball on a summer night.

Yolo, finding me again.

171.

now

Like that poem about the soldier, I've been naming the parts.

Mom.

Dad.

Jack.

Syd.

Sam.

Alex.

Ella.

In my mind, in my heart.

Over and over again for the past year.

Maybe I still don't see them fully or perfectly, even with time, even with hindsight.

But All. I. Want.

Is to see them again.

172.

now

It's dark, but not full dark.
 If I wish, right now, something will happen. It has to.
 I close my eyes.
 I say a name.
 This was always who it was going to be.

173.

now

I've been trying to assign the clues to different people. Syd. Sam. Alex. Jack. Ella. I tried to bend them, to make them match up with who I most wanted to come back right then.

I tried to make them fit anyone.

I tried to make them fit everyone.

174.

now

Hello? I say.
    But
    No one's here.
    They will never be here.
    The only person here
    is me.

175.

now

I am the one at the jump.
I am the one
who came back.

176.

now

I'll tell you what happened that night.
    But it will be a story.
    And remember.
    You should
    always
    look
    very carefully
    at the person
    who tells the story.

177.

now

"I'm here," I say out loud.
  I am the one leaving clues.
  I am the one leaving messages.
  I am still
  the only girl in town.

178.

now

Syd, Sam, my family, Alex, Ella.
They didn't mean to break me that night.
And I didn't jump.
I fell.

179.

now

Not the way you think I fell.
Not into the water.
I fell out of myself.
I fell out of my life.

180.

once, that night

I walked back from the jump alone. Alone, alone. I knew everyone would be okay without me. So I made my way back to the parking lot. The Subaru was there with its apple stickers inside and no one to ride shotgun or in the back seat.

I got in the car.

I was not a person. I was pain in skin.

I told myself all I had to do was get myself home.

And I did.

And I was done.

181.

once, that night

When I got home, I folded in on myself. I could feel my lungs breathing and my heart beating.

Burst, I thought. *Break.*

But it didn't.

I didn't.

182.

now

I have been so scared of impermanence. And change. And loss.

After that night, I thought:

This is how you stay safe.

You go inside yourself.

You lock the door.

You do not leave.

And now I know this, too:

You do not live.

I don't know who I am without sadness anymore. It lives in my heart, my stomach, my limbs, my head, every vein threading through me. And a kind of limbic system of guilt runs along with it. For the mistakes I made, for being the kind of person other people could leave behind and discard.

If you take away the sadness and guilt, I don't know what I am anymore. *Only if I fix them,* I thought, *is there any way to go on being. Only if I hide and stay locked up inside can I possibly keep going.*

But there is no fixing.

And this is not living.

So.

Knowing that.
Is there a way to go on?
Instead of staying in this place alone?

183.

now

I stand alone at the top of the jump.

There is no reason to take off my T-shirt so it will be dry, for later.

No reason for me to take off my running shoes so they don't weigh me down.

No reason for me to do anything
but jump.

And how I jump decides where I will fall
into the water
or onto the rocks.

It's hard to hear someone fall if they don't scream.
But you hear when they hit what's below.

184.

now

It's true what they say about falling.
Time does slow down.
Not much
but enough
to think about
who and what you love.
You don't have time to call them all out loud, but
that doesn't matter.
They are already engraved upon your heart.

185.

now

I hit at the edge of the water. It swallows me cold, whole and deep.

There is still another
choice to make.

186.

now

Do I
    breathe in water
    or
    swim for air.

187.

now

I have done good things and bad things.
   I have tried and given up.
   So.
   The question is.
   Can I do this?
   Living?
   Knowing it will all happen again?
   Not the same things. Not the same pain.
   But with new? And still the old?
   My favorite book says
   there are worse things than dying.
   That's true, of course.
   There is something worse than death.
   It's loneliness.

And I have been

so

absolutely

lonely.

I am July Fielding.

I am a Fall Creek Girl.

I have traveled in a pack. I have traveled alone.

I run faster than fast, harder than hard.

My feet push off the ground. Blood pumps in my veins and pounds in my heart.

I know how to tear up a hill and how to fly when I'm tired.

I run all over town, but there is one run in particular that defines me.

It starts in a gorge that could break me. It doesn't. I run up the stone steps, through the crevice the water has cut. Across the suspension bridge, a thread over the gorge. It is secret and misty. Down a long road, past Flatrock. The sun chases me along that road and through green farmland, rolling hills.

I cut through the wildflower preserve, through the grass and blossoms and rumbling bees, to Fall Creek, where the water is deep and emerald green and the cliffs are darkest gray.

I can live a lifetime in a long run.

This one begins at the jump.

I climb out of the water
    cold and dripping
    and I
    begin to run.

A good run is like a good story. There is a journey—a trail through trees, a field where a tractor has made ruts packed-down and wide enough for a single person to run, stone stairs where you could slip and fall. Birds dart up from the long green and gold grasses dewed in the morning. The early-morning sun gilds the mossy stones, melts away the frost. Your lungs burn, your heart is thudding, your eyes are open to the world. There may be others with you. There may be no one at all.

You do not know how the run will end. There could be victory, defeat, disappointment, elation. There could be a moment where you are about to seize it all and someone you never even saw coming flies past you to claim the victory. You could be behind from the start, have to follow and try to catch someone mile after beaten-down mile.

But the deepest truth about running is that, when you run truly alone, it is not a race, it is not a story.

It is you.

I am running. I am almost home when it happens.

The light from the rising moon is of a particular clarity. In my head, I am singing the *July, July Fielding* song, over and over, to match the rhythm of my gait.

And then I hear

cicadas.

birds.

the hum of people.

A car passes me.

Another.

In this moment I know.

That I am always going to be okay.

And that I will never be okay.

I have felt these things before.

But now I know them. As sure as I know anything.

Both things are true. But one more than the other.

July, July Fielding.

July, July Fielding.

July, July Fielding.

You will be okay.

And as the words come over me and the lights come on in my town, I know that I am not, at this moment, afraid.

We are all so strong. Every day that we do it. Every day that we choose it.

There are cars in the driveway. The sprinklers are snick-hissing. A baseball mitt waits on the lawn, in the square of light from the kitchen window. I hear voices inside. Shadows move behind the shades. A bowl of cat food sits on the steps.

I have told you a story.

I have told myself one, too.

It is true to me.

And this is true, too.

No matter how much you want to,

you can't

get them back.

Instead you

let them go.

And maybe you find

each other again.

I don't know what that looks like.

I don't know what anything looks like

except

I'm not going to stay here alone

anymore.

Who will be there?
   I don't know.
   but
   I open the door
   and
   let them in.